The Legend of the Thunder God

Fairy tales, Folk tales, Legends & Mythology, Volume 4

Patrick William Lee

Published by Starlit Tales Publishing, 2024.

This is a work of fiction. Similarities to real people, places, or events are entirely coincidental.

THE LEGEND OF THE THUNDER GOD

First edition. August 21, 2024.

Copyright © 2024 Patrick William Lee.

ISBN: 979-8227208637

Written by Patrick William Lee.

Table of Contents

To the dreamers who gaze at the stormy skies and find inspiration in the roar of thunder,

To the warriors who fight not just with strength, but with heart, seeking balance in a world of chaos,

And to the storytellers who breathe life into legends, ensuring that the tales of courage, sacrifice, and hope live on through the ages.

This book is for you—may the thunder of your legacy echo across the heavens.

Chapter 1: The Birth of the Thunder God

The Awakening of the Heavens

In the vastness of the universe, before the birth of time as mortals know it, the heavens stirred with an energy so potent it resonated through the very fabric of creation. The cosmic order, which had remained in a delicate balance for eons, was about to shift. Stars flickered with a newfound intensity, and the moons of distant worlds aligned in a way that had not been seen since the beginning of time itself. This was the heralding of a new force, one that would forever alter the destinies of gods and mortals alike—the birth of the Thunder God.

The celestial winds howled as if in anticipation, and the skies darkened, not in foreboding but in preparation for the entrance of one who would wield the very forces of nature. In the heart of the divine realm, atop the sacred Mount Tempest, the council of ancient elemental spirits gathered. These beings, formed from the primordial energies of the world, had existed since the dawn of creation. They were the guardians of the elemental forces—earth, fire, water, and air—and their presence commanded respect from all who dwelled in the heavens.

Each spirit embodied the essence of their respective element. Terra, the spirit of earth, stood tall and sturdy, her form reminiscent of the mountains, unyielding and ancient. Pyra, the spirit of fire, blazed with an intensity that could melt stone, her eyes glowing like molten lava. Aquila, the spirit of water, flowed gracefully, her form ever-changing like the rivers and oceans she governed. Zephyr, the spirit of air, was ethereal, her presence barely visible yet felt in every breath of wind. Together, they formed the council that would oversee the birth of the Thunder God.

As the elemental spirits gathered, a great storm began to brew in the skies above Mount Tempest. Dark clouds rolled in, crackling with electricity, as the winds howled and the ground trembled. The elements themselves were in turmoil, for they sensed the coming of a power that would command them all.

"The time has come," Terra said, her voice a deep rumble that echoed through the mountains. "The prophecy is upon us. The Thunder God is to be born."

"His power will be great," Pyra added, her fiery form flickering with excitement. "But will he wield it with wisdom?"

"That remains to be seen," Aquila replied, her voice like the gentle flow of a stream. "We must guide him, ensure that he understands the balance of the elements."

"The balance must be maintained," Zephyr whispered, her voice carried on the wind. "For without it, chaos will reign."

The council stood in solemn silence as the storm reached its peak. The skies above Mount Tempest split open with a thunderous crack, and a bolt of lightning, brighter than a thousand suns, struck the peak of the mountain. The force of the lightning was so immense that it shattered the rock, sending shards of stone cascading down the mountainside. And from the heart of the storm, a figure emerged.

He was born of lightning and thunder, his form crackling with electricity. His eyes glowed with the intensity of a storm, and his presence commanded the respect of the elements themselves. He was the Thunder God, destined to wield the power of the storms and to bring balance to the world.

As he took his first breath, the storm began to subside, the clouds parting to reveal a clear sky. The elemental spirits approached him, each one offering their guidance and wisdom.

"Welcome, Thunder God," Terra said, her voice warm and reassuring. "You are born of the earth and the sky. Your power is great, but so too is your responsibility."

"Your power can bring life or destruction," Pyra added, her fiery gaze intense. "You must learn to control it, to use it wisely."

"The waters will guide you," Aquila said, her form shimmering like a calm lake. "They will teach you the ways of patience and reflection."

"And the winds will carry you," Zephyr whispered, her voice like a gentle breeze. "They will show you the paths you must take."

The Thunder God listened to the words of the elemental spirits, his mind absorbing their wisdom. He knew that his journey was just beginning and that the path ahead would be filled with challenges and trials. But he also knew that he was not alone, for the elements themselves would be his allies.

The Prophecy Unveiled

In the days that followed the birth of the Thunder God, the heavens were abuzz with anticipation. The prophecy of his coming had been foretold in the ancient scrolls, passed down through generations of gods and spirits. It was said that the Thunder God would rise to power during a time of great turmoil, when the balance of the elements was threatened by forces of chaos.

The prophecy spoke of a figure born of the storm, destined to wield the power of lightning and thunder. He would be the protector of the balance, the one who would restore harmony to the elements. But the prophecy also warned of a great trial, a battle that would determine the fate of the world. The Thunder God would face challenges that would test his strength, his wisdom, and his resolve.

As the Thunder God grew in power, the elemental spirits continued to guide him, teaching him the ways of the elements and the responsibilities that came with his power. They took him to the Hall of Prophecies, a sacred chamber deep within Mount Tempest, where the ancient scrolls were kept. The walls of the chamber were adorned with inscriptions, each one telling the story of a different prophecy.

"The prophecy of your birth is written here," Terra said, gesturing to a scroll that glowed with a faint blue light. "It is your destiny to fulfill it."

The Thunder God approached the scroll, his hand hovering over the ancient parchment. As he touched it, the words on the scroll began to glow brighter, and the room was filled with a soft, humming sound. The prophecy revealed itself to him, the words etching themselves into his mind.

In the time of storms and shadows, when the elements are in disarray, the Thunder God shall be born. From the heart of the storm, he shall rise, wielding the power of the heavens. He shall bring balance to the elements and restore harmony to the world. But beware, for his journey shall be fraught with peril. The forces of chaos shall rise against him, and he shall face a trial that will test his very soul. Only through strength, wisdom, and sacrifice shall he prevail, and his legacy shall be written in the annals of time.

The words of the prophecy resonated within the Thunder God, filling him with a sense of purpose and destiny. He knew that his journey would not be easy, but he was determined to fulfill his role in the balance of the world. The elemental spirits watched as he absorbed the prophecy, their expressions unreadable.

"Your journey begins now," Pyra said, her voice tinged with a mix of pride and concern. "The prophecy has been revealed, and your destiny awaits."

"But remember," Aquila added, her voice gentle but firm, "destiny is not set in stone. It is shaped by your choices, your actions. You have the power to forge your own path."

The Thunder God nodded, his resolve strengthening. He knew that the path ahead would be difficult, but he was ready to face whatever challenges lay in his way. With the elemental spirits by his side, he would fulfill the prophecy and restore balance to the world.

The Celestial Convergence

As the Thunder God prepared to embark on his journey, the heavens themselves seemed to align in his favor. The celestial convergence, a rare and powerful event, was approaching. During this time, the stars and planets would align in perfect harmony, amplifying the powers of the gods and spirits. It was a time of great significance, one that would mark the beginning of the Thunder God's rise to power.

The elemental spirits knew that the celestial convergence was no coincidence. It was a sign that the Thunder God's time had come, that the forces of the universe were aligning to support his journey. But they also knew that the convergence would not go unnoticed by those who sought to disrupt the balance.

"There are those who will see the convergence as an opportunity," Zephyr warned, her voice filled with caution. "They will seek to use its power for their own gain."

"The forces of chaos are always waiting," Terra agreed, her tone grave. "We must be vigilant."

The Thunder God listened to their warnings, understanding the gravity of the situation. He knew that the celestial convergence would be a turning point in his journey, a moment when his true power would begin to manifest. But he also knew that it would attract the attention of those who sought to challenge him.

On the night of the convergence, the Thunder God stood atop Mount Tempest, gazing up at the night sky. The stars were brighter than ever before, their light shimmering like diamonds in the darkness. The planets moved into alignment, their positions creating a perfect symmetry that resonated with the very essence of the universe.

As the celestial bodies converged, the Thunder God felt a surge of energy within him. It was as if the power of the heavens was being channeled directly into his being, amplifying his strength and sharpening his senses. The air crackled with electricity, and the ground beneath him trembled with anticipation.

The elemental spirits stood by his side, their forms glowing with the energy of the convergence.

They watched as the Thunder God embraced the power of the celestial event, his aura expanding with the force of the storm.

"This is your moment," Pyra said, her voice filled with pride. "The convergence has given you the strength you need to face the challenges ahead."

"But use it wisely," Aquila cautioned. "Power is a double-edged sword. It can protect, but it can also destroy."

The Thunder God nodded, understanding the wisdom in her words. He could feel the immense power coursing through him, but he knew that he must wield it with care. The convergence had given him the strength he needed, but it was up to him to use it for the greater good.

As the celestial event reached its peak, a bolt of lightning struck the peak of Mount Tempest, splitting the sky with a deafening roar. The energy of the convergence surged through the Thunder God, and for a moment, time seemed to stand still. He was one with the storm, one with the very forces of nature.

And then, as quickly as it had begun, the convergence ended. The planets moved out of alignment, and the stars returned to their normal brilliance. The energy that had filled the heavens began to dissipate, leaving behind a sense of calm and quiet.

The Thunder God stood in the aftermath of the convergence, his heart filled with a newfound sense of purpose. He knew that his journey was just beginning, but he was ready to face whatever lay ahead. The celestial convergence had marked the beginning of his rise to power, and he would not squander the opportunity it had given him.

The elemental spirits watched him in silence, their expressions a mix of pride and concern. They knew that the Thunder God was destined for greatness, but they also knew that his journey would be fraught with danger. The prophecy had foretold it, and the convergence had set it in motion.

But as the Thunder God stood atop Mount Tempest, gazing out at the vast expanse of the world before him, he felt no fear. He was the Thunder God, born of lightning and thunder, destined to bring balance to the elements. His journey had begun, and he would face whatever challenges lay ahead with courage and determination.

The Council's Decision

With the celestial convergence complete, the council of elemental spirits gathered once more in the Hall of Prophecies. The energy of the convergence still lingered in the air, a reminder of the power that had been unleashed. The Thunder God had proven himself worthy of the prophecy, but the council knew that his journey was far from over.

"The convergence has given him strength," Terra said, her voice filled with admiration. "He is ready to begin his journey."

"But the challenges he will face are great," Pyra replied, her fiery form flickering with concern. "The forces of chaos will not sit idly by."

"We must guide him," Aquila said, her tone resolute. "He is powerful, but he is still young. He will need our wisdom."

"And our protection," Zephyr added, her voice like a gentle breeze. "For there are those who will seek to destroy him."

The council members nodded in agreement. They knew that the Thunder God was destined for greatness, but they also knew that he would need their guidance to navigate the trials ahead. The prophecy had foretold of a great battle, one that would test the very soul of the Thunder God. It was a battle that would determine the fate of the world, and the council was determined to see him through it.

"We shall be his guardians," Terra declared, her voice firm. "We shall guide him, protect him, and ensure that he fulfills his destiny."

The council members placed their hands over the scroll of the prophecy, each one infusing it with their elemental power. The scroll glowed with a brilliant light, the words of the prophecy etched into the very fabric of the world.

"The Thunder God shall rise," Pyra said, her voice filled with conviction. "And we shall stand by his side."

The council's decision was final. They would guide the Thunder God on his journey, helping him to fulfill the prophecy and bring balance to the elements. The path ahead would be difficult, but the council was confident that the Thunder God had the strength and resolve to overcome any challenge.

With the decision made, the council members left the Hall of Prophecies, their forms dissolving into the elements they represented. They would watch over the Thunder God, guiding him from the shadows and ensuring that he remained true to his destiny.

As the Hall of Prophecies returned to its quiet state, the scroll of the prophecy remained, glowing with the combined power of the elemental spirits. It was a symbol of the Thunder God's destiny, a reminder of the journey that lay ahead.

And so, the Thunder God's journey began. With the power of the celestial convergence still fresh within him, and the guidance of the elemental spirits to light his way, he would face the challenges ahead with courage and determination. The prophecy had been set in motion, and the Thunder God was ready to fulfill his destiny.

The Importance of Destiny

As the Thunder God embarked on his journey, he reflected on the words of the prophecy and the guidance of the elemental spirits. He understood that his path was not one of his choosing, but one that had been laid out for him by forces beyond his control. Yet, he did not resent this destiny. Instead, he embraced it, understanding that it was his purpose in life.

The Thunder God knew that destiny was not something to be feared or resisted, but something to be accepted and fulfilled. It was the path that led him to his true purpose, the journey that would define his existence. He understood that every challenge he faced, every battle he fought, was a step toward fulfilling his destiny.

But he also understood that destiny was not a guarantee of success. It was a guide, a path that could be followed or strayed from. The choices he made, the actions he took, would determine whether he fulfilled his destiny or fell short of it. He knew that he had the power to shape his own fate, but that power came with great responsibility.

As he journeyed through the world, the Thunder God encountered many who had strayed from their own destinies, who had chosen paths of greed, hatred, or fear. He saw the consequences of those choices, the suffering and destruction they brought. And he vowed that he would not fall into the same traps.

The Thunder God's journey was not just a quest to fulfill the prophecy, but a journey of self-discovery. He would learn the true meaning of destiny, the importance of accepting one's purpose, and the power of choice. He would come to understand that destiny was not a burden, but a gift—a guide that led him to his true self.

And so, with the prophecy as his guide and the wisdom of the elemental spirits as his compass, the Thunder God set out on his journey. He would face trials and tribulations, battles and betrayals, but he would do so with the knowledge that he was fulfilling his destiny. He was the Thunder God, born of lightning and thunder, destined to bring balance to the elements. His journey had begun, and he would see it through to the end.

Chapter 2: The First Storm

The Child of Storms

The birth of the Thunder God had been a momentous occasion, one that resonated throughout the heavens and the earth. The celestial beings had recognized his arrival, the elemental spirits had guided his first steps, and the prophecy of his destiny had been revealed. But as with all beings, even those of divine origin, the Thunder God had to grow, learn, and come to understand the full extent of his powers. This journey of discovery began in his childhood, a time when innocence often mingled with the stirrings of immense potential.

The Thunder God, known by the name Raijin in his youth, grew up in the ethereal plains of the heavens, a realm where the sky kissed the ground, and clouds formed paths beneath one's feet. Here, the young deity was surrounded by the whispers of the wind, the gentle hum of distant thunder, and the ever-present energy of the storm that seemed to live within him. His early years were spent in exploration and play, his childish curiosity driving him to explore the vast expanses of his home.

Raijin was not like other divine children. While they played with the soft light of the stars or danced with the winds, Raijin felt a deeper, more turbulent energy within himself. His emotions were often mirrored by the skies above; a flash of anger could cause the distant rumble of thunder, and a burst of joy might bring a refreshing shower. These occurrences were small at first, almost unnoticeable, but they hinted at the power that lay dormant within him.

As Raijin grew older, the power within him began to manifest more clearly. He could feel the storm in his veins, the electricity in his fingertips. It was exhilarating, but also frightening. He was a child, after all, and the power he wielded was vast, far beyond his understanding.

One day, while wandering through the cloud forests that bordered the heavenly realm, Raijin found himself alone, surrounded by towering formations of vapor and mist. The air was thick with moisture, and the sky above was dark and heavy, as if it too sensed the power stirring within the young god.

Feeling an unfamiliar restlessness, Raijin stretched out his hand toward the sky, his fingers tingling with the energy that seemed to pulse from deep within him. He closed his eyes, imagining the clouds parting, the wind picking up, and the first drops of rain falling from the heavens. He could see it so clearly in his mind, the storm he could conjure with just a thought.

But as he focused, something unexpected happened. The sky, which had been merely overcast, began to darken rapidly. The clouds thickened, swirling in a vortex above him. The air grew charged with electricity, and the wind began to howl, whipping through the cloud forest with a force that bent the trees and sent leaves spiraling into the air.

Raijin opened his eyes in surprise, feeling the storm respond to his thoughts in a way that he had not intended. He could feel the power building, the energy growing stronger and more uncontrollable by the second. His heart raced, not with excitement, but with fear. The storm was too strong, too wild. It was beyond his control.

He tried to calm himself, to stop the storm, but it was too late. The winds howled louder, the clouds roared with thunder, and the first bolt of lightning cracked across the sky, splitting the heavens with a deafening roar. The ground beneath Raijin shook with the force of the storm, and the air was thick with the scent of ozone.

The storm spirits, ancient beings of the sky, sensed the disturbance and were drawn to the source. They emerged from the swirling clouds, their forms flickering with lightning, their voices the rumble of distant thunder. They were spirits of immense power, born of the same forces that Raijin now struggled to control.

"Young one," the leading spirit boomed, its voice reverberating through the storm. "You dare to summon the storm without understanding its power?"

Raijin stared at the storm spirits, his fear growing as he realized the gravity of what he had done. He had summoned a storm far beyond his ability to control, and now these powerful beings were here to challenge him, to test his worth.

"I...I didn't mean to," Raijin stammered, his voice small and uncertain. "I was just...trying."

The storm spirits circled him, their forms shifting and crackling with energy. They were not cruel, but they were stern, for they knew the danger that unchecked power could bring.

"The storm is not a toy for a child's amusement," another spirit intoned, its voice like the crack of lightning. "It is a force of nature, one that can bring life or destruction."

Raijin felt a wave of shame wash over him. He had not meant to cause harm, but his lack of control had put everything around him at risk. The storm he had summoned was growing stronger by the moment, and he did not know how to stop it.

"Please," he begged, his voice trembling. "Help me. I don't know what to do."

The storm spirits paused, their forms flickering as they considered the young god's plea. They could see that he was not malicious, merely inexperienced and overwhelmed by the power he possessed.

"You must learn to control your power," the leading spirit said finally, its tone softening. "We will guide you, but you must listen, and you must understand."

Raijin nodded, desperate to regain control of the storm he had unleashed. The storm spirits moved closer, their energy intertwining with his, and together they began the process of calming the storm. The wind began to die down, the clouds slowly parted, and the thunder grew quieter until it was little more than a distant rumble.

It was a difficult process, one that required immense concentration and effort, but under the guidance of the storm spirits, Raijin was able to bring the storm under control. The skies cleared, and the air became still once more, leaving Raijin exhausted but relieved.

"You have great power," the leading storm spirit said, its form shimmering as it began to fade. "But with great power comes great responsibility. You must learn to control it, or it will control you."

Raijin nodded, feeling the weight of the spirit's words. He had learned a valuable lesson that day, one that he would carry with him as he grew into his full potential. The power of the storm was immense, but it was not something to be wielded lightly. It required respect, understanding, and above all, responsibility.

As the storm spirits disappeared, leaving Raijin alone in the now-calm cloud forest, he realized that his journey had only just begun. He had taken his first steps toward understanding his power, but there was still much to learn. And he knew that the storm within him would not be tamed easily.

The Elder God's Guidance

The incident with the storm spirits left a deep impression on Raijin. He realized that while he possessed immense power, he lacked the understanding and discipline needed to wield it safely. His encounter with the storm had been a stark reminder that his abilities were not just a source of wonder, but also a potential danger to himself and others.

In the days that followed, Raijin sought guidance from the elder gods, beings of great wisdom who had lived through countless ages. These gods were the keepers of ancient knowledge, and they had seen the rise and fall of many powerful beings. They understood the delicate balance of power and responsibility, and they knew how to guide those who sought to learn.

Among these elder gods was Fujin, the Wind God, an ancient deity who had mastered the elements of air and sky. Fujin was known for his calm demeanor and his deep understanding of the natural forces that shaped the world. He was a mentor to many young gods, helping them to understand the complexities of their powers.

Raijin approached Fujin with humility, seeking the elder god's guidance. He told Fujin of his encounter with the storm spirits, of the storm he had unwittingly unleashed, and of his desire to learn how to control his powers.

Fujin listened patiently, his eyes thoughtful as he considered Raijin's words. He could see the potential in the young Thunder God, but he also saw the uncertainty and fear that came with such immense power.

"You are wise to seek guidance," Fujin said finally, his voice as gentle as a breeze. "Power without understanding is like a storm without direction—it can cause great harm without meaning to."

Raijin nodded, feeling the truth in Fujin's words. He had seen the destruction that an uncontrolled storm could bring, and he did not want to be the cause of such chaos.

"The storm within you is a part of who you are," Fujin continued, "but it is not something to be feared. It is a gift, one that can bring life as well as destruction. The key is to find balance, to understand the nature of your power and to use it with wisdom."

Fujin led Raijin to a high peak, where the winds howled and the skies were clear. The view from the peak was breathtaking, with the world stretched out below them, and the heavens above. It was a place where the elements met, where the forces of nature could be felt in their purest form.

"Here, you will learn the first lesson," Fujin said, his gaze fixed on the horizon. "Close your eyes and feel the wind."

Raijin did as he was told, closing his eyes and focusing on the sensation of the wind against his skin. At first, it was just a gentle breeze, but as he concentrated, he could feel the different currents of air, the subtle shifts in temperature and pressure. He could sense the wind's direction, its speed, and its intent.

"Do not try to control it," Fujin instructed. "

Just feel it, understand it. The wind is a living force, just like the storm. It has its own will, its own purpose. To control it, you must first understand it."

Raijin remained still, letting the wind guide his senses. He began to see the patterns in the air, the way the wind flowed and interacted with the world around him. It was a dance, a delicate balance of forces that created the currents and eddies in the sky.

As he focused, Raijin felt a connection with the wind, a sense of harmony that he had not experienced before. He realized that the wind was not something to be commanded, but something to be worked with. It was a partner, not a servant.

"Good," Fujin said, sensing Raijin's progress. "Now, open your eyes and look at the sky."

Raijin opened his eyes and gazed at the clear blue sky above. It was vast, endless, and full of possibilities. Fujin pointed to a distant cloud, a small wisp of vapor that floated gently across the horizon.

"Focus on that cloud," Fujin instructed. "Feel the energy within you, the power of the storm. But do not force it. Let it flow, like the wind. Guide the storm, but do not try to control it."

Raijin nodded and focused on the cloud, feeling the familiar tingling sensation in his fingers as the energy of the storm began to build within him.

But this time, instead of trying to command the storm, he let the energy flow naturally, guiding it gently toward the cloud.

The sky responded to his touch. The small wisp of cloud began to grow, fed by the energy of the storm. It expanded, darkening slightly as it absorbed the moisture from the air. Raijin could feel the wind shifting around him, supporting the growth of the cloud, helping it to form.

But as the cloud grew, Raijin remained calm, not letting the storm's power overwhelm him. He kept his focus, guiding the storm with a gentle hand, ensuring that it remained in balance with the wind and the sky.

The cloud continued to grow until it was a large, dark cumulus, full of potential but still under control. Raijin could feel the power within it, the energy of the storm ready to be unleashed. But he did not let it go. Instead, he held the storm in check, maintaining the delicate balance between power and control.

"Excellent," Fujin said, his voice filled with approval. "You have learned the first lesson of the storm. Power must be guided, not forced. Control comes from understanding, from working with the forces of nature, not against them."

Raijin smiled, feeling a sense of accomplishment. He had created a storm, but he had done so with wisdom and care. He had not let the power overwhelm him, and he had not let the storm spiral out of control.

"Remember this lesson," Fujin said, placing a hand on Raijin's shoulder. "The storm is a part of you, but it is not all that you are. You are more than just your power. You are a being of choice, of will. Use your power wisely, and you will become a force for good in this world."

Raijin nodded, feeling the truth in Fujin's words. He knew that he still had much to learn, but he also knew that he was on the right path. With Fujin's guidance, he would continue to grow, to understand the nature of his powers, and to fulfill his destiny as the Thunder God.

The Consequences of Power

As Raijin continued his training under Fujin's guidance, he became more confident in his abilities. He learned to summon storms with precision, to control the winds and the rain, and to channel the power of lightning. But with this newfound confidence came a temptation, one that all beings with great power must face—the temptation to use that power without fully considering the consequences.

One day, while exploring the edges of the heavenly realm, Raijin came across a group of young gods and goddesses playing in a field of clouds. They were laughing and chasing each other, their playful energy filling the air with a sense of joy and freedom.

Raijin watched them from a distance, feeling a pang of longing. He had spent so much time training, learning to control his powers, that he had forgotten what it was like to simply play and enjoy life. He wanted to join them, to feel the thrill of carefree fun.

But as he approached, one of the young gods, a boy with the power of fire, noticed him and sneered. "Look, it's the storm boy," he said, his voice dripping with disdain. "Come to show off your big, scary lightning?"

The other children laughed, and Raijin felt a flush of anger. He had worked hard to control his powers, to prove himself, and now they were mocking him. He clenched his fists, feeling the storm stir within him.

"I'm not here to show off," Raijin said, his voice tight. "I just wanted to join in."

"Oh, sure," the fire god said with a smirk. "You're just here to play. Why don't you show us what you can do, storm boy? Let's see if you're really as powerful as they say."

Raijin hesitated, feeling the storm within him growing stronger. He knew that he shouldn't use his powers out of anger, that he should stay in control. But the taunts of the other children stung, and he wanted to prove that he was not someone to be underestimated.

"Fine," Raijin said, his eyes narrowing. "You want to see what I can do? Watch this."

He raised his hand to the sky, summoning the energy of the storm with a force that he had never used before. The sky darkened instantly, and the winds howled as a massive cloud formed above the field. Lightning crackled within the cloud, and the air grew thick with the scent of rain.

The children stopped laughing, their eyes wide with fear as they realized the power that Raijin was unleashing. The fire god's smirk disappeared, replaced by a look of shock as he watched the storm grow in intensity.

But Raijin didn't stop. He was angry, and the storm fed on that anger, growing stronger and more dangerous by the second. The winds whipped through the field, tearing up the clouds and sending the children running for cover.

The fire god tried to summon his own power, but it was no match for the storm. His flames were snuffed out by the wind and rain, leaving him defenseless against the fury of the storm.

Raijin felt a surge of satisfaction as he watched the fire god cower before him. He had proven his power, shown them all that he was not to be mocked. But as the storm continued to rage, he began to realize that he had lost control.

The storm was too strong, too wild. It tore through the field, threatening to destroy everything in its path. The children screamed as they were buffeted by the wind and rain, and Raijin felt a growing sense of dread.

He tried to stop the storm, to calm it as he had done before, but it was too late. The storm had taken on a life of its own, fueled by his anger and pride. It was no longer under his control.

"Help!" the fire god shouted, his voice barely audible over the roar of the storm. "Stop it! Please!"

Raijin's heart sank as he realized the full extent of what he had done. He had let his anger get the better of him, and now his friends were in danger because of it. He had failed to remember the lesson that Fujin had taught him—that with great power comes great responsibility.

Just as Raijin was about to lose hope, he felt a familiar presence beside him. Fujin appeared, his form shimmering with the power of the wind. The elder god's expression was stern, but there was no anger in his eyes, only disappointment.

"Raijin," Fujin said, his voice calm but firm. "This is not the way."

"I'm sorry," Raijin whispered, his voice choked with regret. "I didn't mean to..."

Fujin raised his hand, and the storm began to calm. The winds died down, the clouds parted, and the rain stopped. The field was left in shambles, but the children were safe, if shaken.

The fire god, still trembling from the experience, looked at Raijin with a mixture of fear and awe. "You...you really are powerful," he said, his voice quivering.

Raijin didn't respond. He felt ashamed of what he had done, of how he had let his anger control him. He had wanted to prove his power, but in doing so, he had put others in danger.

Fujin placed a hand on Raijin's shoulder, his gaze gentle but serious. "Power is not something to be used carelessly," he said. "It is a great responsibility, one that must be wielded with wisdom and restraint. You have learned a hard lesson today, but it is an important one."

Raijin nodded, his heart heavy with the weight of his actions. He knew that Fujin was right, that he had let his pride and anger lead him down a dangerous path. He had almost lost control of the storm, and the consequences could have been disastrous.

"I'm sorry," Raijin said again, his voice filled with remorse. "I didn't mean to hurt anyone."

"I know," Fujin replied, his tone softening. "But you must remember that power can be a double-edged sword. It can protect, but it can also harm. The choice of how to use it is yours, and you must choose wisely."

Raijin nodded, understanding the elder god's words. He had been given a great gift, but with it came great responsibility. He could not afford to let his emotions dictate his actions, not when so much was at stake.

As the children slowly returned to the field, their fear beginning to fade, Raijin approached the fire god. He could see the fear in the boy's eyes, and he felt a deep sense of guilt for what he had done.

"I'm sorry," Raijin said sincerely, his voice filled with regret. "I shouldn't have let things get out of hand. I just...wanted to prove that I wasn't weak."

The fire god hesitated, his eyes still wary, but eventually he nodded. "I...I understand," he said quietly. "Just...don't do it again, okay?"

Raijin smiled weakly, grateful for the boy's forgiveness. "I won't," he promised. "I've learned my lesson."

As the children resumed their play, Raijin stood beside Fujin, watching them with a sense of relief. He knew that he still had much to learn, but he also knew that he was on the right path. He had made a mistake, but he had learned from it, and he would not make the same mistake again.

Fujin placed a hand on Raijin's shoulder, his gaze filled with pride. "You have done well today," he said. "You have learned an important lesson, one that will serve you well in the future. Remember this day, and remember the responsibility that comes with your power."

Raijin nodded, feeling a sense of resolve. He knew that his journey was far from over, but he also knew that he was not alone. With Fujin's guidance, he would continue to grow, to learn, and to become the Thunder God that he was destined to be.

As the sun began to set, casting a golden glow over the field, Raijin felt a renewed sense of purpose. He was the Thunder God, born of lightning and thunder, destined to bring balance to the elements. And with each lesson he learned, he was one step closer to fulfilling his destiny.

Chapter 3: The Trial of the Mountains

The Call to the Mountains

The celestial plains of the heavens had been the Thunder God's home since his birth, a place where he learned to harness his powers and began to understand the responsibilities that came with them. Under the guidance of elder gods like Fujin, the Wind God, Raijin had grown stronger and more confident in his abilities. But the time had come for him to face a greater challenge, one that would test not just his strength, but his spirit, resolve, and endurance. It was time for the Trial of the Mountains.

The mountains, ancient and imposing, stood at the edge of the heavenly realm, their peaks reaching into the very fabric of the sky. These mountains were more than mere landforms; they were alive with the essence of the earth and the heavens, a place where the elements converged in their purest forms. It was said that within these mountains resided the Mountain Giants, powerful beings who guarded the ancient secrets of the world. Only those deemed worthy could pass through their domain and learn the wisdom hidden within the stone.

Raijin had heard the tales of the Mountain Giants and the trials they set for those who sought their knowledge. Many had attempted the journey, but few had returned, and those who did were forever changed, their minds and bodies strengthened by the trials they had faced. For Raijin, the call to the mountains was not just a test of his powers; it was a rite of passage, a journey that would prove his worth as the Thunder God.

Fujin, ever the wise mentor, saw the determination in Raijin's eyes and knew that the young god was ready. "The mountains are unforgiving," Fujin warned as they stood at the base of the towering peaks. "They will test you in ways you cannot imagine. Strength alone will not see you through—this trial requires endurance, wisdom, and the will to persevere against all odds."

Raijin nodded, his gaze fixed on the path ahead. The wind howled through the narrow passes, carrying with it the scent of earth and stone. The mountains loomed above him, their peaks hidden by swirling clouds, as if the heavens themselves were guarding the secrets within.

"I understand," Raijin replied, his voice steady. "But I must do this. I must prove to myself that I am worthy of the power I possess."

Fujin placed a hand on Raijin's shoulder, his expression one of pride and concern. "Remember, Raijin, the trial is not just about reaching the summit. It is about the journey itself. Every step you take, every challenge you face, will teach you something about yourself. Trust in your strength, but also in your wisdom."

With those words, Raijin set off on his journey. The path ahead was steep and treacherous, winding through jagged cliffs and narrow ledges. The air grew colder with each step, the wind biting at his skin as he ascended higher into the mountains. But Raijin was undeterred. He had prepared for this moment, honing his body and mind, and he was determined to see it through.

As he climbed, the landscape around him began to change. The trees became sparse, their gnarled branches twisted by the relentless wind. The ground beneath his feet was rough and uneven, a mix of loose gravel and solid rock. The higher he went, the more the mountain seemed to come alive, as if sensing his presence and testing his resolve.

The first challenge came sooner than expected. A narrow pass, barely wide enough for him to squeeze through, lay before him. On either side, the rock walls rose steeply, their surfaces jagged and sharp. The wind whipped through the pass with a ferocity that threatened to knock him off balance, and the path ahead was obscured by mist.

Raijin took a deep breath and steadied himself. He knew that turning back was not an option; he had to push forward, no matter the difficulty. With careful steps, he began to navigate the narrow pass, his hands gripping the rough rock for support. The wind howled around him, tearing at his clothes and hair, but he pressed on, his eyes focused on the path ahead.

Halfway through the pass, the ground beneath him shifted. A loose rock gave way, and Raijin felt himself slipping. Instinctively, he reached out, grabbing hold of a jagged outcrop to steady himself. The sudden movement sent a sharp pain through his hand, but he ignored it, pulling himself back onto the path.

For a moment, he paused to catch his breath, his heart pounding in his chest. The wind seemed to grow louder, as if mocking his near-fall. But Raijin refused to be intimidated. He had come too far to be deterred by a mere slip.

With renewed determination, he continued through the pass, each step more careful than the last.

Finally, after what felt like an eternity, he emerged from the narrow pass onto a wider ledge. The wind was still strong, but the path was more stable, giving him a moment to rest. He looked back at the pass, now shrouded in mist, and felt a sense of accomplishment. It was a small victory, but it was a reminder that he could overcome the challenges before him.

But the mountain was far from finished with him.

The Mountain Giants

As Raijin continued his ascent, the landscape grew more rugged, the air thinner and colder. The path became less defined, forcing him to rely on his instincts to find his way. He could feel the weight of the journey beginning to take its toll on his body, but he pushed through the fatigue, knowing that the true test was yet to come.

After several hours of climbing, Raijin reached a plateau, a flat expanse of rock that seemed out of place in the otherwise steep and jagged terrain. The air was still, the wind having died down as if in anticipation of what lay ahead. In the center of the plateau stood a massive stone gate, its surface etched with ancient symbols that glowed faintly in the dim light.

Raijin approached the gate, his footsteps echoing in the stillness. He could sense the power emanating from the gate, a deep, ancient energy that resonated with the very core of the mountain. As he drew closer, the symbols on the gate began to glow brighter, pulsing with a rhythm that matched his heartbeat.

Without warning, the ground beneath him shook, and the stone gate began to rumble. Raijin stepped back, watching in awe as the gate slowly opened, revealing a dark passage beyond. From the shadows emerged three towering figures, their forms massive and imposing, their eyes glowing with an otherworldly light.

The Mountain Giants.

These beings were the guardians of the mountains, ancient spirits of the earth who had existed since the beginning of time. Their bodies were made of stone and earth, their skin rough and weathered, their movements slow but deliberate. They towered over Raijin, their presence filling the plateau with a sense of overwhelming power.

The largest of the giants stepped forward, its eyes narrowing as it regarded Raijin with a mixture of curiosity and caution. "Who dares to enter our domain?" the giant's voice boomed, the sound reverberating through the mountain.

Raijin straightened, meeting the giant's gaze with unwavering resolve. "I am Raijin, the Thunder God," he declared, his voice steady. "I seek the wisdom of the mountains and the trials that will prove my worth."

The giant's eyes gleamed with interest. "The Thunder God, you say? We have heard of you, child of storms. But know this—our trials are not for the faint of heart. Many have come before you, seeking the secrets of the mountains, but few have succeeded."

"I am prepared," Raijin replied, his determination unwavering. "I will face whatever trials you set before me."

The giant studied him for a long moment, its expression unreadable. Then, with a nod, it stepped aside, gesturing for Raijin to enter the passage beyond the gate. "Very well, Thunder God. The trials await you. But be warned—these mountains do not show mercy. You will be tested in ways you cannot imagine, and only the strongest will prevail."

Raijin took a deep breath and stepped forward, passing through the stone gate and into the dark passage. The Mountain Giants watched him go, their eyes glowing in the dim light. They knew that the trials ahead would be difficult, but they also sensed something in Raijin—a strength, a resolve that set him apart from those who had come before.

As Raijin ventured deeper into the passage, the light from the entrance faded, leaving him in near-total darkness. The air was cold and heavy, and the walls of the passage seemed to close in around him. But Raijin did not falter. He knew that the only way to prove his worth was to press on, no matter how difficult the journey became.

The First Trial: The Path of Endurance

The passage eventually opened into a vast cavern, its walls lined with jagged rocks and sharp stalactites that hung like the teeth of a great beast. The ground was uneven, littered with loose stones that shifted underfoot, making each step treacherous. At the far end of the cavern, Raijin could see a narrow path that wound its way upward, disappearing into the shadows above.

As Raijin approached the path, he felt a sudden rush of wind, followed by a low, rumbling growl that echoed through the cavern. The ground beneath him shook, and Raijin steadied himself, his senses on high alert. He knew that this was the first trial—the Path of Endurance.

The path was narrow and steep, with barely enough room for Raijin to place his feet. The walls of the cavern loomed close on either side, their rough surfaces scraping against his skin as he carefully navigated the treacherous terrain. The wind howled through the cavern, cold and relentless, tearing at his clothes and hair.

Raijin gritted his teeth and pressed on, each step requiring immense focus and effort. The path seemed to stretch on forever, winding upward in a series of sharp turns and steep inclines. His muscles burned with exertion, his lungs struggled for breath in the thin air, but he refused to give in to the fatigue.

As he climbed, the wind grew stronger, pushing against him with increasing force. It seemed to come from all directions at once, making it difficult to keep his balance. At times, the wind was so strong that it nearly knocked him off the path, forcing him to cling to the rough walls for support.

But Raijin was determined. He had come too far to be defeated by the wind. He called upon the energy within him, the power of the storm, and used it to steady himself. He became one with the wind, allowing it to guide him rather than resist it.

Slowly but surely, Raijin made his way up the path, his body and mind pushed to their limits. The journey was grueling, each step more difficult than the last, but he persevered, driven by the knowledge that this was only the beginning of the trial. He knew that the true challenge lay ahead, and he would need every ounce of strength to overcome it.

Finally, after what felt like an eternity, Raijin reached the top of the path. The narrow trail opened onto a wide ledge, and he collapsed to his knees, his body trembling with exhaustion. The wind had died down, leaving the cavern eerily silent.

But Raijin knew better than to let his guard down. He forced himself to his feet, his legs shaking with the effort. He had passed the first part of the trial, but the real test was yet to come.

At the far end of the ledge, a massive stone door stood embedded in the rock wall. The door was adorned with ancient symbols, similar to those on the gate at the entrance to the mountains. Raijin approached the door cautiously, his senses alert for any sign of danger.

As he reached out to touch the door, the symbols began to glow, and the door slowly creaked open. Beyond the door lay a dark tunnel, its walls lined with glowing crystals that pulsed with a soft, blue light. Raijin took a deep breath and stepped inside, the door closing behind him with a heavy thud.

The Second Trial: The Labyrinth of Shadows

The tunnel led Raijin into a vast underground labyrinth, a maze of twisting passages and narrow corridors that seemed to stretch on endlessly. The walls of the labyrinth were made of dark stone, their surfaces smooth and cold to the touch. The glowing crystals provided the only light, casting eerie shadows that danced on the walls.

Raijin knew that this was the second trial—the Labyrinth of Shadows. It was a test of his resolve and his ability to navigate the unknown. The labyrinth was said to be alive, shifting and changing to confuse and disorient those who entered. Many had become lost in its depths, never to be seen again.

But Raijin was undeterred. He knew that he had to keep moving, to trust his instincts and find a way through the maze. He began to walk, his footsteps echoing in the silence. The air was thick with the scent of earth and stone, and the only sound was the steady rhythm of his breathing.

As he ventured deeper into the labyrinth, the passages became narrower, the walls closing in around him. The shadows grew darker, their shapes twisting and contorting into unsettling forms. Raijin could feel the weight of the darkness pressing down on him, but he refused to let fear take hold. He had faced greater challenges before, and he would not be defeated by shadows.

But the labyrinth was more than just a physical challenge—it was a test of his mind and spirit. The shadows seemed to whisper to him, their voices soft and insidious, filling his mind with doubt and fear. They taunted him, reminding him of his failures, his insecurities, the times when he had faltered.

Raijin clenched his fists, trying to block out the voices. He knew that they were not real, that they were just tricks of the labyrinth, but the doubts they stirred were all too familiar. He had always struggled with the weight of his responsibilities, the fear that he would not live up to the expectations placed upon him.

The shadows seemed to sense his hesitation, their whispers growing louder and more persistent. They showed him visions of his past failures—the storm he had unleashed in anger, the times when he had lost control of his power, the moments when he had doubted himself. The darkness threatened to overwhelm him, to consume him whole.

But Raijin refused to give in. He knew that this was the true test of the labyrinth—to see if he could overcome his own fears and doubts. He forced himself to focus, to remember the lessons he had learned from Fujin and the other elder gods. He had the strength within him, the power to overcome any challenge, if only he believed in himself.

With renewed determination, Raijin pressed on through the labyrinth, ignoring the whispers and the shadows that clawed at his mind. He followed the glowing crystals, using them as a guide through the twisting passages. The labyrinth continued to shift and change, but Raijin was no longer afraid. He had faced his inner demons and emerged stronger for it.

After what felt like hours of wandering, Raijin finally reached the center of the labyrinth. There, in a small chamber, he found a pool of crystal-clear water, its surface still and calm. The water glowed with a soft, ethereal light, illuminating the chamber with a peaceful radiance.

Raijin approached the pool and knelt beside it, his reflection staring back at him from the water's surface. He could see the exhaustion in his eyes, the toll that the trials had taken on him, but he also saw something else—strength, resolve, and a newfound sense of purpose.

The water seemed to call to him, and without hesitation, Raijin reached out and touched the surface. The moment his fingers made contact, the water began to ripple, and a soft voice echoed through the chamber.

"You have done well, Raijin," the voice said, its tone gentle and soothing. "You have faced the shadows within yourself and emerged victorious. But your journey is not yet complete. The final trial awaits you."

Raijin nodded, understanding that the voice was that of the mountain itself, a manifestation of the ancient wisdom that resided within. He knew that the final trial would be the most difficult of all, but he was ready. He had come this far, and he would not turn back now.

The water in the pool began to swirl, and a narrow staircase emerged from its depths, leading downward into the earth. Raijin took a deep breath and descended the staircase, the light from the pool fading as he ventured into the darkness below.

The Final Trial: The Heart of the Mountain

The staircase led Raijin into a vast underground chamber, its walls made of smooth, polished stone that gleamed in the faint light of the glowing crystals embedded in the ceiling. The chamber was eerily silent, the air thick with a sense of ancient power. In the center of the chamber stood a massive stone pedestal, upon which rested a large, glowing crystal.

Raijin approached the pedestal, his heart pounding in his chest. He could feel the immense energy radiating from the crystal, a power unlike anything he had ever encountered before. This was the heart of the mountain, the source of its ancient wisdom and the key to completing the final trial.

But as Raijin reached out to touch the crystal, the ground beneath him shook, and the walls of the chamber began to tremble. The air grew heavy with tension, and Raijin sensed that something was coming, something powerful and dangerous.

Without warning, the stone floor split open, and from the depths of the earth emerged a massive figure, its form towering over Raijin. It was a Mountain Giant, but unlike the ones he had encountered before, this one was made entirely of glowing, molten rock. Its eyes burned with an intense, fiery light, and its voice rumbled like an earthquake.

"You have come far, Raijin, but your final challenge awaits," the giant boomed, its voice filling the chamber. "To prove your worth, you must defeat me and claim the heart of the mountain. Only then will you be worthy of the ancient wisdom it holds."

Raijin steeled himself, knowing that this would be the most difficult battle he had ever faced. The giant was made of pure energy, its body radiating heat and power that made the air around it shimmer. But Raijin knew that he could not back down. He had come too far to fail now.

The giant let out a roar, and the chamber was filled with a blinding light as it charged toward Raijin. The ground shook with each step, and the heat from the giant's body was almost unbearable. But Raijin stood his ground, calling upon the power of the storm within him.

With a shout, Raijin unleashed a bolt of lightning, striking the giant square in the chest. The impact caused the giant to stumble, but it quickly regained its footing and retaliated with a massive swing of its molten fist. Raijin barely managed to dodge the blow, the heat from the giant's fist singeing his clothes.

The battle raged on, the chamber filled with the sounds of thunder and the roar of the giant. Raijin used all of his strength and skill to evade the giant's attacks while launching his own, but the giant was relentless, its fiery form seemingly impervious to the lightning strikes.

Raijin knew that he could not win this battle through brute force alone. He needed to find a way to outsmart the giant, to use its own power against it. As he dodged another swing of the giant's fist, an idea began to form in his mind.

He remembered the lessons he had learned from Fujin—the importance of balance, of working with the elements rather than against them. The giant was made of molten rock, a combination of fire and earth, but it was also vulnerable to the elements that created it.

Raijin called upon the wind, summoning a powerful gust that whipped through the chamber, fanning the flames of the giant's body. The wind intensified, feeding the fire within the giant and causing it to burn hotter and brighter. The heat became unbearable, and the giant let out a roar of frustration as its own flames began to consume it.

But Raijin did not stop there. He summoned the rain, calling down a torrential downpour that filled the chamber with steam as it struck the molten rock. The giant's fiery form began to cool, the molten rock solidifying into brittle stone. The giant roared in anger, its movements growing slower and more labored as the rain continued to fall.

Finally, Raijin unleashed a massive bolt of lightning, striking the giant with all the force he could muster. The lightning struck the giant's chest, shattering the brittle stone and sending cracks spiderwebbing across its body. With a final roar, the giant crumbled, its fiery light fading as it fell to the ground in a pile of broken rock.

Raijin stood panting, his body trembling with exhaustion. The chamber was silent once more, the only sound the steady drip of water from the ceiling. He had done it—he had defeated the giant and completed the final trial.

With the giant defeated, the glowing crystal on the pedestal began to pulse with light, filling the chamber with a soft, ethereal glow. Raijin approached the pedestal, his heart filled with a sense of accomplishment and relief. He reached out and touched the crystal, feeling its warmth and energy flow through him.

In that moment, the chamber was filled with a deep, resonant voice, the voice of the mountain itself. "You have proven yourself, Raijin, Thunder God. You have faced the trials of the mountains and emerged victorious. The ancient wisdom of the earth and sky is now yours."

Raijin closed his eyes, feeling the knowledge of the mountains flow into him. He saw visions of the earth and sky, of the elements in perfect harmony, of the balance that must be maintained to keep the world in order. He understood the connection between the earth and the heavens, the way the mountains served as a bridge between the two, a place where the forces of nature converged.

When the visions faded, Raijin opened his eyes, feeling a deep sense of peace and understanding. He had completed the trials, but more importantly, he had learned the true value of perseverance, of inner strength, and of the wisdom that came from overcoming adversity.

With the crystal in hand, Raijin began his journey back to the surface, the path now clear before him. As he emerged from the mountains and into the light of the heavenly realm, he felt a renewed sense of purpose. He had proven his worth, not just to the Mountain Giants, but to himself.

The Trial of the Mountains was over, but Raijin knew that his journey was far from complete. There would be more challenges ahead, more trials to face, but he was ready. He was the Thunder God, and he would continue to grow in strength and wisdom, forging his path toward fulfilling his destiny.

As Raijin stood at the edge of the mountains, looking out over the vast expanse of the world below, he felt a deep connection to the earth and the sky. He understood now that his power was not just a gift, but a responsibility—a responsibility to maintain the balance of the elements and to protect the world from those who would seek to disrupt it.

With a final glance at the mountains behind him, Raijin turned and began his journey back to the heavenly realm, the lessons of the trials etched into his heart and mind. He knew that he had much to learn, but he also knew that he had the strength and determination to overcome any challenge that lay ahead.

The Trial of the Mountains had tested him in ways he had never imagined, but it had also made him stronger, more resilient, and more aware of the true nature of his power. And as he walked away from the mountains, Raijin knew that he was one step closer to fulfilling his destiny as the Thunder God.

Chapter 4: The Encounter with the Serpent

The Stirring of Chaos

The Thunder God, Raijin, had faced many trials in his journey, from the harrowing Trial of the Mountains to the lessons taught by the elder gods. He had grown in strength and wisdom, learning to control the immense power that coursed through his veins. Yet, as with all journeys of self-discovery and growth, new challenges awaited him—challenges that would test not only his strength but also his understanding of the world and his role within it.

The heavens had been peaceful for many years, a period of calm and balance that the gods worked diligently to maintain. But beneath the surface of this harmony, a force had been brewing—one that threatened to unravel the very fabric of the world. It was a force as old as time itself, a manifestation of chaos that sought to disrupt the order that the gods had established.

This force took the form of a mighty serpent, a creature of immense power and malevolence. The serpent was born from the primordial chaos that existed before the world was formed, a remnant of the wild, untamed energies that once ruled the cosmos. It had slumbered for eons, buried deep within the earth, waiting for the moment when it could rise and reclaim its dominion.

The serpent was not merely a creature of physical might; it embodied the very essence of chaos. Its presence warped the natural order, causing storms to rage uncontrollably, rivers to flow backward, and the earth to tremble. The balance between the elements, carefully maintained by the gods, began to falter as the serpent stirred, awakening from its long slumber.

The first signs of the serpent's awakening were subtle—small disturbances in the natural world that only the keenest observers would notice. The winds shifted unpredictably, carrying with them the scent of something ancient and malevolent. The skies darkened at odd times, and the stars themselves seemed to flicker, as if disturbed by a presence that should not be.

Raijin, ever attuned to the forces of the storm, was one of the first to sense the growing imbalance. He could feel it in the air, a tension that made the hairs on the back of his neck stand on end. The storms he summoned were no longer as responsive to his commands; they grew wild and erratic, as if something was interfering with the natural order.

Concerned by these disturbances, Raijin sought counsel from Fujin, the Wind God, who had guided him through many of his earlier trials. Fujin, too, had noticed the shifts in the balance and had grown uneasy.

"The winds whisper of a great disturbance," Fujin said, his voice tinged with worry as he and Raijin stood atop a high peak, overlooking the vast expanse of the world below. "A force of chaos has awakened, one that threatens to undo the balance we have worked so hard to maintain."

Raijin nodded, his brow furrowed in thought. "I have felt it too. The storms are not as they should be, and the elements are in disarray. What could be causing this?"

Fujin's gaze turned toward the distant horizon, where dark clouds gathered ominously. "There is an ancient legend," he began, his voice low, "of a serpent that once ruled the world before the gods brought order to the chaos. It was a creature of immense power, born of the primordial void. The serpent was defeated and sealed away deep within the earth, where it was to slumber for all eternity. But legends also speak of a time when the serpent would awaken, and chaos would once again threaten the world."

Raijin felt a chill run down his spine at Fujin's words. The serpent—an embodiment of chaos itself—had awakened, and it was up to him to stop it before it could bring ruin to the world.

"Where can I find this serpent?" Raijin asked, his voice steady despite the gravity of the situation.

Fujin turned to face Raijin, his expression solemn. "The serpent's lair lies in the heart of the earth, in a place where the elements converge and the balance is most delicate. It is a place of great power, but also of great danger. If you seek to confront the serpent, you must be prepared for the battle of your life."

Raijin nodded, his resolve firm. "I will face the serpent, and I will restore the balance. The world depends on it."

With Fujin's guidance, Raijin set off on his journey to the serpent's lair. He knew that this battle would not be like any he had faced before. The serpent was a creature of pure chaos, and defeating it would require not just strength, but a deep understanding of the balance between chaos and order.

The Journey to the Lair

The path to the serpent's lair was fraught with peril. Raijin traveled across vast landscapes, each more treacherous than the last. The world itself seemed to react to the serpent's awakening, as if nature was trying to repel him from reaching his destination.

Raijin crossed deserts where the sands shifted like water, swirling into deadly whirlwinds that threatened to swallow him whole. He traversed forests where the trees twisted and writhed, their branches reaching out like claws to ensnare him. The skies above him were filled with dark clouds that crackled with uncontrolled lightning, the storms no longer under his command.

But Raijin pressed on, undeterred by the challenges before him. He knew that the serpent's presence was growing stronger with each passing day, and the longer it remained unchecked, the more the world would fall into chaos. He had to reach the lair before it was too late.

As Raijin journeyed deeper into the heart of the earth, he encountered creatures that had been twisted and corrupted by the serpent's influence. These were beings of the natural world—animals, spirits, and even minor gods—who had been drawn to the serpent's chaotic power and transformed into monstrous versions of their former selves.

One such creature was a massive wolf, its fur black as night and its eyes glowing with an unnatural light. The wolf had once been a guardian spirit of the forest, but now it prowled the land as a creature of pure destruction, driven mad by the serpent's influence.

Raijin encountered the wolf as he made his way through a dense forest, the trees closing in around him like the bars of a cage. The air was thick with the scent of decay, and the ground was littered with the bones of animals that had fallen prey to the wolf.

The wolf emerged from the shadows, its growl low and menacing as it circled Raijin. Its eyes were filled with madness, and its jaws dripped with the blood of its recent kills.

Raijin stood his ground, summoning the power of the storm within him. He knew that the wolf was not truly evil, but a victim of the serpent's chaos. Still, it was a threat that could not be ignored.

As the wolf lunged at him, Raijin unleashed a bolt of lightning, striking the creature with a force that sent it crashing to the ground. But the wolf was not easily defeated. It rose to its feet, shaking off the attack as if it were nothing more than a minor inconvenience.

Raijin realized that brute force alone would not be enough to defeat the wolf. He needed to find a way to break the serpent's hold on the creature, to restore it to its true form.

As the wolf charged at him again, Raijin focused on the energy within the beast. He could feel the serpent's influence, a dark and chaotic force that had twisted the wolf's spirit. With great concentration, he reached out with his own power, trying to push back the serpent's influence and free the wolf from its grip.

The struggle was intense, a battle of wills that took place on a level beyond the physical. Raijin could feel the serpent's power resisting him, trying to tighten its hold on the wolf. But Raijin did not give up. He knew that the balance between chaos and order was at stake, and he had to succeed.

Finally, with a great effort, Raijin managed to break the serpent's hold on the wolf. The creature let out a pained howl as the dark energy was expelled from its body, leaving it weakened and disoriented.

Raijin approached the wolf cautiously, his hand outstretched in a gesture of peace. The wolf, now free of the serpent's influence, looked up at him with clear eyes. It no longer posed a threat; instead, it was a spirit in need of healing.

"Rest now," Raijin said softly, placing his hand on the wolf's head. "The chaos has been driven out."

The wolf let out a soft whine before collapsing to the ground, its body fading into the earth as its spirit returned to the forest. The trees around them seemed to sigh with relief, the oppressive atmosphere lifting as the serpent's influence was removed.

Raijin knew that this was just one of many creatures that had fallen victim to the serpent's chaos. As he continued his journey, he encountered more twisted beings—each one a reminder of the serpent's growing power and the urgency of his mission.

The Serpent's Lair

After many days of travel, Raijin finally reached the entrance to the serpent's lair. The lair was hidden deep within a massive mountain range, its entrance guarded by jagged cliffs and treacherous paths. The air was thick with the scent of sulfur, and the ground beneath his feet was hot to the touch, as if the very earth was boiling with the serpent's presence.

The entrance to the lair was a massive cavern, its walls lined with glowing crystals that pulsed with a sickly green light. The crystals were remnants of the serpent's influence, their once-pure energy now corrupted by the chaos that emanated from the creature within.

Raijin knew that this was the point of no return. Once he entered the lair, he would be face-to-face with the serpent, and there would be no turning back. He took a deep breath, summoning the full strength of the storm within him, and stepped into the cavern.

The lair was vast, a sprawling network of tunnels and chambers that seemed to stretch on endlessly. The air was thick with the serpent's presence, a palpable force that made it difficult to breathe. Raijin could feel the weight of the chaos pressing down on him, but he pushed forward, determined to reach the heart of the lair.

As he made his way deeper into the lair, the tunnels grew narrower, the walls closing in around him. The glowing crystals became more numerous, their light pulsing in time with the serpent's heartbeat. The ground beneath his feet was uneven, and the air was filled with the sound of dripping water and distant echoes.

Finally, Raijin reached the central chamber of the lair. The chamber was enormous, its ceiling so high that it was lost in darkness. In the center of the chamber, coiled around a massive stone pillar, was the serpent.

The creature was colossal, its body stretching hundreds of feet in length. Its scales were as black as the void, shimmering with a dark, oily sheen. Its eyes were like twin suns, glowing with an intense, fiery light that seemed to burn with the very essence of chaos. The serpent's mouth was filled with razor-sharp fangs, and its tongue flicked out, tasting the air as it sensed Raijin's presence.

The serpent uncoiled itself from the pillar, its massive body slithering across the floor of the chamber with a sound like grinding stone. It raised its head, towering over Raijin, and let out a low, rumbling hiss that shook the very walls of the lair.

Raijin stood his ground, his eyes locked on the serpent. He could feel the creature's immense power, a force of chaos that threatened to overwhelm him. But he knew that he could not back down. The balance of the world was at stake, and he had to confront the serpent and restore order.

The serpent reared back, preparing to strike. Raijin braced himself, summoning the full power of the storm within him. Lightning crackled around his body, and the air was filled with the sound of thunder as he prepared to face the serpent in battle.

The Battle of Chaos and Order

The serpent struck with blinding speed, its massive jaws snapping shut just inches from Raijin's head. Raijin leaped to the side, narrowly avoiding the attack, and countered with a bolt of lightning that struck the serpent's side.

The serpent let out a roar of pain, but it was far from defeated. It whipped its tail around, sending a wave of force toward Raijin that shattered the ground beneath him. Raijin was thrown backward, crashing into the wall of the chamber with a force that left him momentarily dazed.

But Raijin was not so easily defeated. He pushed himself to his feet, his eyes blazing with determination, and unleashed a torrent of lightning and wind that engulfed the serpent. The chamber was filled with the deafening roar of thunder and the blinding flash of lightning as Raijin poured all of his power into the attack.

The serpent writhed and thrashed, its body contorting as it fought against the storm. But the creature was resilient, its chaotic nature allowing it to withstand the onslaught. The serpent let out a roar, its eyes glowing with an even greater intensity, and countered with a blast of dark energy that tore through the storm and struck Raijin with a force that sent him crashing to the ground.

Raijin gasped for breath, his body aching from the impact. The serpent loomed over him, its eyes burning with malevolent fury. The creature's power was overwhelming, a force of pure chaos that threatened to consume everything in its path.

But Raijin knew that he could not give up. He had faced countless trials and challenges, and each one had made him stronger, more resilient. He had learned the value of perseverance, of pushing through even when the odds seemed insurmountable. And he knew that this battle was about more than just defeating the serpent—it was about restoring the balance between chaos and order.

With a roar of determination, Raijin pushed himself to his feet and unleashed a surge of power that sent shockwaves through the chamber. The storm around him intensified, the winds howling with fury as they tore at the serpent's body. Lightning crackled through the air, striking the serpent with the force of a thousand storms.

But the serpent was not easily defeated. It fought back with everything it had, its chaotic energy clashing with Raijin's power in a battle that shook the very foundations of the world. The chamber was filled with the sound of thunder and the roar of the serpent as the two forces clashed, each trying to overpower the other.

As the battle raged on, Raijin realized that brute force alone would not be enough to defeat the serpent. The creature was a manifestation of chaos itself, and it could not be destroyed through sheer power. Instead, Raijin needed to find a way to restore the balance, to bring order to the chaos that the serpent embodied.

He remembered the lessons he had learned from Fujin, the importance of balance and harmony in the natural world. The serpent was a force of chaos, but chaos was not inherently evil—it was a necessary part of the world, just as order was. The key was to find the right balance between the two, to ensure that neither chaos nor order became too dominant.

With this realization, Raijin changed his approach. Instead of trying to overpower the serpent, he began to channel his energy into restoring the balance. He used his power to calm the storm, to bring order to the chaos that surrounded him. The winds died down, the lightning ceased, and the chamber grew quiet as Raijin focused on restoring harmony.

The serpent, sensing the change in Raijin's tactics, hesitated. It could feel the balance shifting, the chaotic energy that fueled it beginning to wane. The creature let out a low hiss, its eyes narrowing as it watched Raijin closely.

Raijin stepped forward, his voice calm and steady as he addressed the serpent. "You are a creature of chaos, but chaos and order must exist in harmony. Without balance, the world cannot thrive. I do not seek to destroy you, but to restore the balance that has been lost."

The serpent's eyes flickered with uncertainty, its massive body coiled tightly as it considered Raijin's words. For a moment, the creature seemed to waver, its chaotic energy pulsing erratically.

Raijin extended his hand, his palm glowing with a soft, blue light. "Let us restore the balance together," he said, his voice filled with conviction. "Chaos and order, working in harmony for the good of the world."

The serpent stared at Raijin, its eyes glowing with an intense light. The chamber was silent, the air thick with tension as the two forces stood at a crossroads.

Finally, after what felt like an eternity, the serpent began to uncoil. Its eyes softened, the fiery glow fading as the chaotic energy within it began to calm. The creature lowered its head, acknowledging Raijin's words and accepting the balance that he sought to restore.

Raijin stepped forward, placing his hand on the serpent's head. The blue light from his palm spread through the serpent's body, enveloping the creature in a soothing, calming energy. The chamber was filled with a soft, harmonious hum as the balance between chaos and order was restored.

The serpent let out a low, rumbling sigh, its body relaxing as the chaotic energy within it was brought into harmony with the natural order. The creature's scales shimmered with a new light, a reflection of the balance that had been achieved.

Raijin smiled, feeling a deep sense of peace and accomplishment. The battle was over, and the balance had been restored. The serpent, once a force of pure chaos, was now a part of the natural order, a guardian of the harmony between chaos and order.

As the serpent slithered back to its place around the stone pillar, Raijin turned to leave the chamber. He knew that his work was not yet done—there were still many challenges and trials ahead. But he also knew that he had taken an important step in his journey, one that had taught him the true nature of his power and his role in maintaining the balance of the world.

The Wisdom of Balance

As Raijin left the serpent's lair, he felt a renewed sense of purpose. The battle with the serpent had taught him an important lesson—one that would guide him in the trials to come. The balance between chaos and order was essential for harmony in the world, and it was his duty as the Thunder God to maintain that balance.

The world was a delicate tapestry, woven from the threads of chaos and order. Too much of one would lead to destruction, while too much of the other would lead to stagnation. The key was to find the right balance, to ensure that both forces could coexist in harmony.

Raijin understood now that his power was not just a weapon, but a tool for maintaining balance. The storms he commanded, the lightning he wielded, were all part of the natural order, and it was his responsibility to use them wisely.

As he journeyed back to the heavenly realm, Raijin reflected on the wisdom he had gained from the encounter with the serpent. He knew that the world would always be in a state of flux, with chaos and order constantly vying for dominance. But he also knew that it was his role to be the guardian of that balance, to ensure that neither force became too powerful.

The serpent had been a formidable opponent, but it had also been a teacher. Through their battle, Raijin had come to understand the true nature of chaos and order, and the importance of maintaining harmony between the two. He had learned that power alone was not enough to bring about change—it required wisdom, understanding, and a deep respect for the balance of the world.

With this newfound wisdom, Raijin was ready to face whatever challenges lay ahead. He knew that there would be more battles, more trials, but he was confident in his ability to overcome them. He was the Thunder God, a guardian of the balance, and he would continue to grow in strength and wisdom, fulfilling his destiny and protecting the world from the forces that threatened it.

As he reached the edge of the mountains, Raijin looked back at the serpent's lair, now quiet and peaceful. The balance had been restored, and the world was once again in harmony. But he knew that his journey was far from over. There were still many lessons to be learned, many challenges to face, and he was ready for whatever the future held.

With a final glance at the mountains, Raijin turned and began his journey back to the heavenly realm, the wisdom of balance etched into his heart and mind. He knew that the world depended on him, and he was determined to fulfill his role as the Thunder God, a protector of the balance between chaos and order.

Chapter 5: The Quest for the Sacred Hammer

The Legend of the Sacred Hammer

In the days following his encounter with the serpent of chaos, Raijin, the Thunder God, felt a new sense of purpose. The battle had taught him invaluable lessons about balance and the importance of harmony between chaos and order. Yet, he also knew that the challenges he had faced so far were just the beginning. Dark forces still lingered, and more trials awaited him. It was in this time of contemplation and reflection that Raijin learned of a powerful artifact—the Sacred Hammer.

The Sacred Hammer was no ordinary weapon. Forged in the primordial fires of creation, it was said to possess the ability to amplify the powers of any who wielded it. Legends spoke of the hammer's might, how it could summon storms of unprecedented fury, split mountains, and control the very elements themselves. Yet, despite its immense power, the hammer had been lost to time, hidden away in a secret location known only to a select few.

It was said that only the most worthy could wield the Sacred Hammer. Many had sought it over the centuries, but none had succeeded in claiming it. The legends also spoke of the hammer's guardians—elemental beings of immense power who protected the weapon from those who were unworthy. Each guardian represented a different elemental force, and together they formed a formidable barrier to any who dared to seek the hammer.

As Raijin learned more about the Sacred Hammer, he found himself drawn to the idea of finding it. He knew that with the hammer in his possession, his powers as the Thunder God would be amplified, allowing him to better protect the balance of the world. But more than that, he felt a deep, almost instinctual pull toward the hammer, as if it was somehow meant to be a part of his destiny.

Raijin sought the counsel of Fujin, the Wind God, who had guided him through many trials before. Fujin listened carefully as Raijin explained his desire to find the Sacred Hammer, his eyes filled with concern.

"The Sacred Hammer is a powerful artifact," Fujin said, his voice calm and measured. "But it is not a weapon to be sought lightly. The legends speak of great trials that must be overcome to claim it, and the hammer itself will only choose a wielder who is truly worthy."

"I understand the risks," Raijin replied, his determination evident. "But I believe that the hammer can help me fulfill my role as the Thunder God. If I am to protect the balance of the world, I must be as strong as possible."

Fujin nodded, sensing Raijin's resolve. "Very well," he said. "But remember this—true power does not come from the weapon you wield, but from the strength of your heart. The Sacred Hammer will not make you invincible; it will only amplify the power that already resides within you. If you seek the hammer for the wrong reasons, it will reject you."

Raijin took Fujin's words to heart, understanding the wisdom behind them. He knew that his quest for the Sacred Hammer was not just about gaining more power; it was also a journey of self-discovery, a test to see if he was truly worthy of wielding such a weapon.

With Fujin's blessing, Raijin set out on his quest to find the Sacred Hammer. He knew that the journey ahead would be long and difficult, filled with trials that would test his strength, courage, and wisdom. But he was determined to see it through, for the sake of the world and the balance he had sworn to protect.

The Journey Begins

Raijin's journey took him across vast and varied landscapes, each more challenging than the last. He traveled through dense forests where the trees towered above him, their branches woven together like a protective canopy. He crossed treacherous deserts where the sun beat down mercilessly, and the sands shifted like waves beneath his feet. He climbed steep mountains that seemed to scrape the sky, their peaks shrouded in mist and mystery.

Along the way, Raijin encountered many obstacles, but he overcame them with the skills and knowledge he had gained from his previous trials. He used the power of the storm to clear his path, summoning lightning to break through barriers and calling upon the wind to lift him over chasms. Yet, despite the challenges, Raijin remained focused on his goal—the Sacred Hammer.

As Raijin journeyed deeper into the wilderness, he began to sense a change in the atmosphere. The air grew thicker, charged with a powerful energy that seemed to emanate from the very earth itself. The sky above darkened, and the winds began to howl with an intensity that Raijin had not felt before. He knew that he was getting closer to the hammer, but he also knew that the trials ahead would be the most difficult yet.

After many days of travel, Raijin arrived at the entrance to a vast, ancient temple. The temple was carved into the side of a mountain, its massive stone doors covered in intricate symbols and runes. The air around the temple was heavy with power, and Raijin could feel the presence of the hammer within.

But as he approached the temple, the ground beneath him began to shake. The doors of the temple slowly creaked open, revealing a long, dark corridor that seemed to stretch on endlessly. Raijin took a deep breath, steeling himself for whatever lay ahead, and stepped inside.

The corridor was dimly lit by torches that flickered with an otherworldly light. The walls were lined with ancient carvings that depicted scenes of battles and triumphs, each one telling the story of those who had sought the Sacred Hammer before him. Some had succeeded in reaching the hammer, but most had fallen to the trials that awaited them.

As Raijin made his way through the corridor, he felt a growing sense of anticipation. He knew that the guardians of the hammer were waiting for him, each one a powerful elemental being who would test his worthiness. He also knew that these trials would not be easy, but he was ready to face whatever challenges lay ahead.

Finally, after what felt like hours of walking, Raijin reached the end of the corridor. Before him stood a massive stone chamber, its walls lined with pillars that seemed to stretch up to the heavens. In the center of the chamber, resting on a pedestal of pure crystal, was the Sacred Hammer.

The hammer was even more magnificent than Raijin had imagined. Its handle was made of a metal that gleamed like the surface of a stormy sea, and its head was adorned with intricate runes that glowed with a soft, blue light. The air around the hammer crackled with energy, and Raijin could feel its power resonating with his own.

But before Raijin could approach the hammer, the ground beneath him began to tremble once more. The pillars surrounding the chamber shook, and from the shadows emerged four towering figures—each one a guardian of the Sacred Hammer, representing a different elemental force.

The Guardians of the Hammer

The first guardian to step forward was a being of fire, its body composed entirely of flames that danced and flickered with an intensity that made the air around it shimmer with heat. The fire guardian's eyes burned with a fierce light, and its voice crackled like the roar of a wildfire.

"I am Ignis, the Guardian of Fire," the being declared, its voice filling the chamber. "To claim the Sacred Hammer, you must first prove that you can withstand the fury of the flames. Only those with the strength to endure the heat of the forge can wield such a weapon."

Raijin nodded, understanding that this was the first of many trials he would face. He knew that fire was a powerful force, one that could bring both destruction and creation. To pass this trial, he would need to show that he could harness the power of fire without being consumed by it.

Ignis raised its fiery hand, and the chamber was suddenly filled with flames. The heat was intense, almost unbearable, but Raijin stood his ground, calling upon the power of the storm to protect him. The air around him crackled with electricity as he summoned a barrier of lightning, shielding himself from the flames.

But Ignis was not easily deterred. The fire guardian intensified the flames, sending waves of heat and fire toward Raijin with a force that threatened to overwhelm him. The temperature in the chamber soared, and the very air seemed to ignite with the intensity of the fire.

Raijin gritted his teeth, focusing all of his energy on maintaining the lightning barrier. He could feel the heat searing his skin, the flames licking at the edges of his barrier, but he refused to back down. He knew that this was a test not just of his strength, but of his resolve and determination.

As the flames continued to rage, Raijin felt a surge of power within him. He realized that the fire was not just an enemy to be defeated, but a force that he could harness and control. With this understanding, he began to channel the energy of the flames into his own power, using the heat to fuel the storm within him.

The lightning barrier around Raijin intensified, glowing brighter and stronger as it absorbed the energy of the fire. The flames that had once threatened to consume him now became a source of strength, amplifying his power and allowing him to stand firm against Ignis's onslaught.

Finally, after what felt like an eternity, Ignis lowered its hand, the flames in the chamber gradually dying down. The fire guardian's eyes flickered with approval as it regarded Raijin.

"You have proven your strength," Ignis said, its voice crackling with a hint of admiration. "You have harnessed the power of fire and turned it into your ally. You may pass this trial."

Raijin nodded, feeling a sense of accomplishment as Ignis stepped back, allowing him to move forward. But he knew that the trials were far from over—three more guardians remained, each one representing a different elemental force.

The next guardian to step forward was a being of water, its form fluid and ever-changing, like the surface of a calm lake one moment and a raging river the next. The water guardian's voice was soft and melodic, like the gentle flow of a stream.

"I am Aqua, the Guardian of Water," the being said, its voice echoing through the chamber. "To claim the Sacred Hammer, you must prove that you can navigate the currents of the mind and spirit. Only those who can remain calm and focused in the face of adversity can wield such a weapon."

Raijin understood that this trial would be different from the one before. While Ignis had tested his physical strength and endurance, Aqua would test his mental and emotional fortitude. Water was a symbol of fluidity and adaptability, and to pass this trial, Raijin would need to show that he could remain calm and clear-headed in the face of challenges.

Aqua raised its hand, and the chamber was suddenly filled with water. The walls and floor disappeared, replaced by an endless expanse of deep, dark water that stretched out in all directions. Raijin found himself floating in the middle of the vast ocean, the surface calm and still.

But the calm was deceptive. Without warning, the water began to churn, waves rising and falling with increasing intensity. The once-still ocean became a turbulent sea, the waves crashing against each other with a force that threatened to pull Raijin under.

Raijin struggled to stay afloat, the powerful currents tugging at him from all sides. The water was cold and unforgiving, its depths dark and foreboding.

But Raijin knew that panicking would only make things worse. He needed to stay calm and focus on finding a way out of the turbulent sea.

He closed his eyes, focusing on his breathing and calming his racing heart. The storm within him began to settle, and he reached out with his senses, trying to understand the currents around him. He realized that the water was not his enemy—it was a force that could be navigated, if he could find the right balance.

Raijin began to move with the currents, allowing the waves to carry him rather than fighting against them. He became one with the water, his movements fluid and graceful as he navigated the turbulent sea. The waves no longer threatened to pull him under; instead, they became a path that guided him forward.

As Raijin continued to navigate the currents, the water began to calm, the waves gradually subsiding until the sea was once again still and serene. He opened his eyes to find himself back in the stone chamber, Aqua standing before him with a look of approval.

"You have proven your wisdom," Aqua said, its voice as calm as the still waters. "You have navigated the currents of the mind and spirit, showing that you can remain focused and clear-headed in the face of adversity. You may pass this trial."

Raijin nodded, feeling a deep sense of inner peace as Aqua stepped back, allowing him to move forward. Two trials were behind him, but two more guardians remained.

The third guardian to step forward was a being of earth, its form solid and imposing, like a mountain that had stood for millennia. The earth guardian's voice was deep and resonant, like the rumble of a distant earthquake.

"I am Terra, the Guardian of Earth," the being declared, its voice filling the chamber. "To claim the Sacred Hammer, you must prove that you have the strength and resilience of the earth itself. Only those who can endure the weight of the world can wield such a weapon."

Raijin understood that this trial would test his physical and emotional resilience. Earth was a symbol of stability and endurance, and to pass this trial, Raijin would need to show that he could withstand immense pressure without breaking.

Terra raised its hand, and the chamber was suddenly filled with the sound of shifting stone. The ground beneath Raijin's feet began to shake, and massive stone pillars rose from the floor, surrounding him on all sides. The pillars moved slowly, their immense weight pressing down on Raijin as they closed in around him.

Raijin felt the weight of the stone pressing down on him, his legs trembling with the effort of holding his ground. The pressure was immense, and every muscle in his body screamed with the strain. But Raijin knew that he could not give in—he needed to stand firm and endure the trial.

He drew upon the strength of the earth itself, grounding himself in the solid stone beneath his feet. The storm within him calmed, and he focused on finding his center, allowing the strength of the earth to flow through him. He could feel the weight of the stone pressing down on him, but he refused to yield, standing tall and firm like a mountain that would not be moved.

The stone pillars continued to press in, their weight crushing, but Raijin remained resolute. He knew that this trial was not just about physical strength—it was about resilience, the ability to endure even the most difficult challenges without breaking.

Finally, after what felt like an eternity, the pressure began to ease. The stone pillars slowly receded, their weight lifting from Raijin's shoulders. He stood tall and unbowed, his body aching but unbroken.

Terra regarded Raijin with a nod of approval, its deep voice filled with respect. "You have proven your resilience," the earth guardian said. "You have withstood the weight of the world, showing that you possess the strength and endurance needed to wield the Sacred Hammer. You may pass this trial."

Raijin nodded, his heart filled with pride and determination as Terra stepped back, allowing him to move forward. Three trials were behind him, and only one guardian remained.

The final guardian to step forward was a being of air, its form ethereal and ever-changing, like a gust of wind that could not be seen or touched. The air guardian's voice was soft and whispering, like the gentle rustle of leaves in a breeze.

"I am Zephyr, the Guardian of Air," the being said, its voice carrying on the wind. "To claim the Sacred Hammer, you must prove that you can navigate the unseen forces that shape the world. Only those who can master the subtle currents of the air can wield such a weapon."

Raijin understood that this trial would test his ability to adapt and respond to the unseen forces that influenced the world. Air was a symbol of change and movement, and to pass this trial, Raijin would need to show that he could navigate the invisible currents that guided the world.

Zephyr raised its hand, and the chamber was suddenly filled with a powerful wind. The air around Raijin began to swirl, creating a vortex that lifted him off the ground and carried him into the air. The wind was strong and unpredictable, buffeting Raijin from all sides as it twisted and turned.

Raijin struggled to regain his balance, the wind tossing him around like a leaf in a storm. He knew that he needed to find a way to navigate the air currents, to regain control of his movements and master the wind.

He closed his eyes, focusing on the subtle shifts in the air around him. He could feel the currents of the wind, the way they moved and flowed in response to the forces around them. He realized that the wind was not something to be controlled—it was something to be understood and navigated.

Raijin began to move with the wind, allowing the currents to guide him rather than fighting against them. He became one with the air, his movements fluid and graceful as he navigated the invisible forces that shaped the world. The wind no longer tossed him around; instead, it carried him forward, lifting him higher and higher.

As Raijin continued to navigate the air currents, the wind began to calm, the vortex gradually subsiding until he was once again standing on solid ground. He opened his eyes to find himself back in the stone chamber, Zephyr standing before him with a look of approval.

"You have proven your adaptability," Zephyr said, its voice as soft as a breeze. "You have mastered the subtle currents of the air, showing that you can navigate the unseen forces that shape the world. You may pass this trial."

Raijin nodded, feeling a deep sense of satisfaction as Zephyr stepped back, allowing him to move forward. The four trials were complete, and Raijin had proven himself worthy in the eyes of the guardians. But there was one final test remaining—the Sacred Hammer itself.

The Final Test

With the four guardians standing aside, Raijin approached the Sacred Hammer. The weapon was even more magnificent up close, its power radiating from it like the warmth of the sun. Raijin could feel the hammer's energy resonating with his own, and he knew that this was the moment he had been preparing for.

But as he reached out to grasp the hammer's handle, a powerful force pushed him back. The hammer's energy flared, creating a barrier of light that prevented him from touching it. Raijin understood that this was the final test—the hammer would not allow itself to be wielded by anyone who was not truly worthy.

Raijin took a deep breath, centering himself and focusing on the lessons he had learned throughout his journey. He remembered Fujin's words—true power lies not in the weapon, but in the heart of the wielder. The Sacred Hammer would not make him invincible; it would only amplify the power that already resided within him.

Raijin knew that he needed to prove himself not just in strength, but in spirit. He needed to show that he was worthy of wielding the hammer, not because of the power it would give him, but because of the responsibility he carried as the Thunder God.

With this understanding, Raijin stepped forward once more. He reached out with his heart, not just his hand, and called upon the strength of his convictions, the wisdom he had gained, and the balance he had learned to maintain. He knew that the hammer was not just a weapon—it was a symbol of the power that came from within, the power to protect and preserve the balance of the world.

As Raijin's hand made contact with the hammer's handle, the barrier of light faded, and the hammer's energy surged through him. The power of the Sacred Hammer resonated with his own, amplifying it and creating a bond that was unbreakable. Raijin could feel the storm within him intensify, the lightning crackling with renewed strength, the wind howling with a fury that was both exhilarating and humbling.

He lifted the Sacred Hammer, its weight solid and reassuring in his hand. The runes on the hammer's head glowed with a bright, blue light, and Raijin knew that he had passed the final test. The hammer had accepted him as its wielder, not because of his strength, but because of the strength of his heart.

The four guardians stepped forward, their eyes filled with pride and respect. Ignis, Aqua, Terra, and Zephyr bowed before Raijin, acknowledging his worthiness as the wielder of the Sacred Hammer.

"You have proven yourself, Raijin, Thunder God," Ignis said, its voice filled with admiration. "You have passed the trials of the elements and shown that you possess the strength, wisdom, and balance needed to wield the Sacred Hammer. May you use it to protect the balance of the world and uphold the responsibilities that come with your power."

Raijin nodded, feeling a deep sense of gratitude and purpose. He knew that his journey was far from over, but he also knew that he had taken an important step toward fulfilling his destiny. With the Sacred Hammer in his hand, he was ready to face whatever challenges lay ahead, confident in the knowledge that true power came not from the weapon, but from the heart of the one who wielded it.

As Raijin left the temple, the Sacred Hammer by his side, he felt a renewed sense of determination. The trials had tested him in ways he had never imagined, but they had also taught him invaluable lessons about the nature of power and the importance of balance. He knew that the challenges ahead would be even greater, but he was ready to face them with the strength and wisdom he had gained.

With the Sacred Hammer as his ally, Raijin continued on his journey, determined to protect the balance of the world and fulfill his role as the Thunder God. The path ahead was uncertain, but Raijin knew that as long as he remained true to himself and the lessons he had learned, he would be able to overcome any obstacle and achieve his destiny.

Chapter 6: The Battle of the Elements

The Gathering Storm

In the aftermath of claiming the Sacred Hammer, Raijin, the Thunder God, felt a deep sense of accomplishment and newfound power. The hammer, forged in the primordial fires of creation, had amplified his abilities, making him more formidable than ever before. But with this power came new responsibilities, and Raijin knew that his journey was far from over. The balance of the world still hung in the balance, and he had much to learn about his role as the guardian of that balance.

As Raijin continued his travels, he sensed a growing tension in the natural world. The elements, once in harmony, seemed to be at odds with each other. Storms brewed in the skies without warning, rivers overflowed their banks, and the earth shook with unnatural tremors. It was as if the very fabric of nature was unraveling, and Raijin could feel the discord in the air.

Raijin sought out Fujin, the Wind God, who had been his mentor and guide through many trials. Together, they stood atop a high mountain peak, looking out over the world below. The sky was dark with storm clouds, and the wind howled with an intensity that made it difficult to stand.

"The elements are in turmoil," Fujin said, his voice barely audible over the roar of the wind. "There is a disturbance in the natural order, and it threatens to tear the world apart."

Raijin nodded, his expression serious. "I can feel it too. The balance has been disrupted, but I don't understand why. What could be causing this?"

Fujin turned to Raijin, his eyes filled with concern. "There are other elemental deities, each one representing a different force of nature. Like you, they are guardians of the natural world, tasked with maintaining the balance of their respective elements. But something has caused them to turn against each other, and now their powers are clashing, creating chaos in the world."

Raijin felt a surge of anxiety. He had always understood the importance of balance, but he had never imagined that the elemental deities themselves could be at odds. "What can I do?" he asked, his voice tinged with worry. "How can I restore the balance?"

"You must face them," Fujin replied, his voice steady. "But this is not a battle of strength alone. You must show them the power of unity and cooperation. The elements are interconnected, and only by working together can they achieve harmony. You must help them see this, or the world will be consumed by chaos."

Raijin knew that Fujin was right. The elements were not separate forces, but parts of a greater whole, and their harmony was essential for the balance of the world. But convincing the other elemental deities of this truth would not be easy, especially when they were already locked in conflict.

With a deep breath, Raijin prepared himself for what lay ahead. He knew that this would be one of the greatest challenges he had ever faced, but he was determined to restore the balance and protect the world from the chaos that threatened it.

The First Confrontation: Ignis, the Fire God

Raijin's first destination was the heart of a vast, arid desert where the Fire God, Ignis, held dominion. The landscape was a sea of red sand, and the air shimmered with heat. The sun blazed down mercilessly, turning the desert into an inferno. It was a land where fire reigned supreme, and the very earth seemed to burn with an intense heat.

As Raijin approached the center of Ignis's domain, he could feel the power of the Fire God growing stronger. Flames danced across the sand, and the air was filled with the crackling of burning wood. In the distance, a massive volcano loomed, its peak glowing with molten lava. This was the heart of Ignis's power, and Raijin knew that the Fire God would not be easily swayed.

At the base of the volcano, Raijin found Ignis standing tall and imposing, his body composed entirely of flames that flickered and roared with an intensity that made the air around him shimmer. Ignis's eyes burned with a fierce light, and his voice crackled like the roar of a wildfire.

"Raijin," Ignis greeted, his tone filled with both respect and challenge. "What brings the Thunder God to my domain? Have you come to test your strength against the flames?"

"I have not come to fight, Ignis," Raijin replied, his voice steady despite the heat that pressed down on him. "I have come to restore the balance. The elements are in turmoil, and it is tearing the world apart. We must work together to bring harmony back to the natural order."

Ignis let out a booming laugh, the flames of his body flaring with intensity. "Work together? With whom? The other elemental deities? They are weak, Raijin. Their powers pale in comparison to the might of the flames. Fire is the force of creation and destruction, and it will consume all that stands in its way."

Raijin shook his head, refusing to be intimidated by Ignis's arrogance. "Fire is powerful, but it is not the only force in the world. The elements must work together, or the balance will be lost. If we do not cooperate, the world will be consumed by chaos."

Ignis's eyes narrowed, the flames of his body burning hotter. "You speak of cooperation, but I see only weakness in your words. If you wish to prove your point, then face me in battle. Show me the power of your storms, and we shall see if your talk of balance holds any weight."

Raijin knew that there was no avoiding a confrontation with Ignis. The Fire God was too consumed by his own power to listen to reason, and the only way to reach him was through battle. But Raijin also knew that this fight was not about defeating Ignis—it was about showing him the importance of cooperation and the interconnectedness of the elements.

With a deep breath, Raijin summoned the power of the storm within him. The sky above darkened as storm clouds gathered, and the air was filled with the crackle of lightning. The ground beneath his feet trembled as thunder rumbled in the distance.

Ignis responded in kind, his flames flaring with a fiery intensity. The sand around him ignited, turning the desert into a sea of fire. The heat was almost unbearable, and the very air seemed to burn with the power of the Fire God.

The battle began with a deafening clash of forces. Raijin unleashed a torrent of lightning, striking the ground around Ignis and sending shockwaves through the desert. The flames roared in response, consuming the sand and turning it into molten glass. The air was filled with the sound of crackling fire and rolling thunder as the two elemental deities clashed.

Raijin knew that he could not defeat Ignis through sheer force. The Fire God was too powerful, and his flames were fueled by the very heart of the earth. Instead, Raijin focused on controlling the storm, using the wind and rain to contain the flames and prevent them from spreading.

But Ignis was relentless, his flames growing hotter and more intense with each passing moment. The heat was suffocating, and Raijin could feel his strength waning as the battle dragged on. He needed to find a way to reach Ignis, to show him that fire was not the only force in the world.

With a surge of determination, Raijin called upon the power of the wind, using it to fan the flames in a controlled manner. The wind carried the flames higher into the sky, where they met with the storm clouds above. As the fire and storm combined, Raijin could feel the energy of the two elements merging, creating a powerful force that was greater than either one alone.

The flames roared with renewed intensity, but instead of consuming everything in their path, they began to dance in harmony with the storm. The fire and lightning intertwined, creating a dazzling display of light and energy that filled the sky. Raijin guided the storm, using the wind to control the flames and direct their power.

Ignis watched in awe as the fire and storm merged into a single, harmonious force. For the first time, he saw the power of cooperation between the elements, the strength that came from unity rather than domination. The flames of his body flickered, their intensity diminishing as he began to understand the truth of Raijin's words.

"You are right, Raijin," Ignis said, his voice filled with a newfound respect. "Fire is powerful, but it is not invincible. The elements must work together if we are to maintain the balance of the world. I see that now."

Raijin nodded, feeling a sense of relief as the flames around them began to subside. "Thank you, Ignis. The world needs us to work together, not against each other. Only then can we restore the balance and protect the natural order."

With Ignis's agreement, the first battle was won. But Raijin knew that his journey was far from over. There were still other elemental deities to face, and he could only hope that they, too, would see the importance of cooperation.

The Second Confrontation: Aqua, the Water Goddess

Leaving the desert behind, Raijin traveled to the realm of Aqua, the Water Goddess. Her domain was a vast expanse of ocean, stretching as far as the eye could see. The sky above was clear and blue, and the waters were calm, reflecting the light of the sun like a mirror.

Raijin stood on the shore, gazing out at the endless sea. He knew that Aqua was one of the most powerful elemental deities, her control over the waters giving her dominion over the tides, rivers, and all bodies of water. The ocean was her domain, and she was its master.

As Raijin stepped into the water, the surface rippled, and Aqua emerged from the depths. Her form was graceful and fluid, her body made of water that shimmered in the sunlight. Her eyes were a deep, tranquil blue, and her voice was as soothing as the gentle flow of a stream.

"Raijin," Aqua greeted, her tone calm and measured. "What brings you to my domain? Have you come to disturb the peace of the waters with your storms?"

"I have come to restore the balance, Aqua," Raijin replied, his voice steady. "The elements are in conflict, and it is causing chaos in the world. We must work together to bring harmony back to the natural order."

Aqua's expression remained serene, but there was a hint of skepticism in her eyes. "The waters are calm, Raijin. The tides flow as they always have, and the rivers follow their courses. There is no conflict here."

"But there is conflict in the world," Raijin insisted. "The elements are not separate forces—they are interconnected, and what happens in one domain affects the others. If we do not work together, the balance will be lost, and the world will suffer."

Aqua regarded Raijin with a thoughtful gaze, the waters around her swirling gently. "I understand your concerns, Raijin, but I see no reason to involve myself in the affairs of other elements. The waters are my responsibility, and they remain in harmony."

Raijin knew that Aqua was not easily swayed. The Water Goddess was known for her calm and measured approach, but she was also fiercely protective of her domain. He needed to show her that the elements were interconnected, and that cooperation was necessary to maintain the balance of the world.

"Aqua," Raijin said, his tone earnest, "the ocean is vast, but it is not isolated. The waters are influenced by the wind, the tides are guided by the moon, and the rivers are fed by the rain. The elements are all connected, and if one is disrupted, the others will be affected. We must work together to protect the balance."

Aqua's eyes softened, but she remained cautious. "You speak of interconnectedness, Raijin, but the waters are my domain. I have no desire to involve myself in the conflicts of the other elements. The ocean is peaceful, and I intend to keep it that way."

Raijin realized that words alone would not convince Aqua. He needed to show her the reality of the interconnectedness of the elements, to demonstrate how the balance of the world depended on their cooperation.

With a deep breath, Raijin raised the Sacred Hammer, summoning the power of the storm. The sky above darkened as storm clouds gathered, and the wind began to howl with increasing intensity. The calm waters of the ocean began to churn, and the surface rippled with the force of the storm.

Aqua watched in surprise as the once-tranquil sea was transformed into a raging tempest. The waves rose higher and higher, crashing against each other with a force that shook the very earth. The winds howled, and the rain began to pour down in sheets, turning the ocean into a maelstrom of chaos.

"Aqua, this is the reality of the world," Raijin called out, his voice barely audible over the roar of the storm. "The elements are interconnected, and when one is disrupted, the others are affected. We must work together to restore the balance, or the world will be consumed by chaos."

Aqua looked out at the raging storm, her expression one of deep contemplation. She could see the truth in Raijin's words—the ocean, once calm and peaceful, had been thrown into turmoil by the forces of the storm. The waters, once under her control, were now at the mercy of the wind and rain.

With a determined look, Aqua raised her hands, summoning the power of the waters. The waves began to calm, and the storm gradually subsided. The winds died down, and the rain ceased, leaving the ocean once again still and serene.

Aqua turned to Raijin, her eyes filled with a newfound understanding. "You are right, Raijin. The elements are interconnected, and we must work together to maintain the balance of the world. I see now that the waters cannot remain isolated from the other elements. We must cooperate to protect the natural order."

Raijin nodded, feeling a sense of relief as Aqua stepped forward, extending her hand in a gesture of unity. "Thank you, Aqua. The world needs us to work together, not against each other. Only then can we restore the balance and protect the natural order."

With Aqua's agreement, the second battle was won. Raijin knew that his journey was nearing its end, but there were still other elemental deities to face. He could only hope that they, too, would see the importance of cooperation.

The Third Confrontation: Terra, the Earth Goddess

Leaving the ocean behind, Raijin traveled to the realm of Terra, the Earth Goddess. Her domain was a vast and fertile land, filled with towering mountains, dense forests, and rolling plains. The earth was rich and abundant, providing life and sustenance to all who lived upon it.

Raijin stood at the base of a towering mountain, looking up at the rocky peaks that seemed to touch the sky. He knew that Terra was one of the most powerful elemental deities, her control over the earth giving her dominion over all that grew and thrived upon it. The mountains, forests, and plains were her domain, and she was their guardian.

As Raijin climbed the mountain, the ground beneath his feet rumbled with the power of the earth. The rocks shifted and cracked, and the air was filled with the scent of fresh soil and growing plants. At the summit of the mountain, Raijin found Terra standing tall and imposing, her body composed of stone and earth that seemed to pulse with life.

Terra's eyes were a deep, earthy brown, and her voice was as steady and unyielding as the mountains themselves. "Raijin," she greeted, her tone calm and measured. "What brings you to my domain? Have you come to disturb the peace of the earth with your storms?"

"I have come to restore the balance, Terra," Raijin replied, his voice steady. "The elements are in conflict, and it is causing chaos in the world. We must work together to bring harmony back to the natural order."

Terra regarded Raijin with a thoughtful gaze, the ground beneath her feet shifting and rumbling with her power. "The earth is strong, Raijin. It provides life and sustenance to all who live upon it. There is no conflict here."

"But there is conflict in the world," Raijin insisted. "The elements are not separate forces—they are interconnected, and what happens in one domain affects the others. If we do not work together, the balance will be lost, and the world will suffer."

Terra's expression remained calm, but there was a hint of skepticism in her eyes. "The earth is resilient, Raijin. It has withstood the test of time and will continue to do so. I see no reason to involve myself in the affairs of the other elements."

Raijin knew that Terra was not easily swayed. The Earth Goddess was known for her strength and stability, but she was also fiercely protective of her domain. He needed to show her that the elements were interconnected, and that cooperation was necessary to maintain the balance of the world.

"Terra," Raijin said, his tone earnest, "the earth is strong, but it is not isolated. The soil is nourished by the rain, the plants are fed by the sun, and the mountains are shaped by the wind. The elements are all connected, and if one is disrupted, the others will be affected. We must work together to protect the balance."

Terra's eyes softened, but she remained cautious. "You speak of interconnectedness, Raijin, but the earth is my domain. I have no desire to involve myself in the conflicts of the other elements. The land is fertile, and I intend to keep it that way."

Raijin realized that words alone would not convince Terra. He needed to show her the reality of the interconnectedness of the elements, to demonstrate how the balance of the world depended on their cooperation.

With a deep breath, Raijin raised the Sacred Hammer, summoning the power of the storm. The sky above darkened as storm clouds gathered, and the wind began to howl with increasing intensity. The ground beneath Raijin's feet rumbled, and the very earth seemed to tremble with the force of the storm.

Terra watched in surprise as the once-stable earth was transformed into a chaotic landscape. The ground cracked and shifted, and the mountains trembled as the storm raged above. The winds howled, and the rain began to pour down in sheets, turning the fertile land into a quagmire of mud and debris.

"Terra, this is the reality of the world," Raijin called out, his voice barely audible over the roar of the storm. "The elements are interconnected, and when one is disrupted, the others are affected. We must work together to restore the balance, or the world will be consumed by chaos."

Terra looked out at the chaotic landscape, her expression one of deep contemplation. She could see the truth in Raijin's words—the earth, once stable and fertile, had been thrown into turmoil by the forces of the storm. The land, once under her control, was now at the mercy of the wind and rain.

With a determined look, Terra raised her hands, summoning the power of the earth. The ground began to calm, and the storm gradually subsided. The winds died down, and the rain ceased, leaving the land once again stable and fertile.

Terra turned to Raijin, her eyes filled with a newfound understanding. "You are right, Raijin. The elements are interconnected, and we must work together to maintain the balance of the world. I see now that the earth cannot remain isolated from the other elements. We must cooperate to protect the natural order."

Raijin nodded, feeling a sense of relief as Terra stepped forward, extending her hand in a gesture of unity. "Thank you, Terra. The world needs us to work together, not against each other. Only then can we restore the balance and protect the natural order."

With Terra's agreement, the third battle was won. Raijin knew that his journey was nearing its end, but there was still one more elemental deity to face. He could only hope that the final confrontation would bring the cooperation and unity needed to restore the balance of the world.

The Final Confrontation: Zephyr, the Wind God

Leaving the mountains behind, Raijin traveled to the realm of Zephyr, the Wind God. His domain was the vast and open sky, where the winds blew freely and the clouds drifted across the horizon. The air was crisp and clear, and the sky was a deep, endless blue.

Raijin stood at the edge of a high cliff, looking out at the vast expanse of the sky. He knew that Zephyr was one of the most elusive elemental deities, his control over the winds giving him the ability to move with the swiftness of a breeze and the power of a hurricane. The sky was his domain, and he was its master.

As Raijin stepped off the cliff, the wind caught him, lifting him into the air. He soared through the sky, carried by the currents of the wind. The air was filled with the scent of fresh grass and blooming flowers, and the sound of the wind rushing past his ears was like music.

In the distance, Raijin saw Zephyr, his form shifting and changing with the wind. Zephyr's body was composed of swirling air, his movements graceful and fluid. His eyes were a pale, ethereal blue, and his voice was as soft and whispering as the breeze.

"Raijin," Zephyr greeted, his tone light and playful. "What brings you to my domain? Have you come to dance with the winds?"

"I have come to restore the balance, Zephyr," Raijin replied, his voice steady. "The elements are in conflict, and it is causing chaos in the world. We must work together to bring harmony back to the natural order."

Zephyr regarded Raijin with a curious gaze, the wind around him swirling gently. "The winds are free, Raijin. They blow where they will, and they do not concern themselves with the affairs of the earth or the sea. There is no conflict here."

"But there is conflict in the world," Raijin insisted. "The elements are not separate forces—they are interconnected, and what happens in one domain affects the others. If we do not work together, the balance will be lost, and the world will suffer."

Zephyr's expression remained light, but there was a hint of skepticism in his eyes. "The winds are swift and changeable, Raijin. They do not stay in one place for long, and they do not concern themselves with the affairs of others. I see no reason to involve myself in the conflicts of the other elements."

Raijin knew that Zephyr was not easily swayed. The Wind God was known for his free-spirited nature, but he was also fiercely protective of his domain. He needed to show Zephyr that the elements were interconnected, and that cooperation was necessary to maintain the balance of the world.

"Zephyr," Raijin said, his tone earnest, "the wind is free, but it is not isolated. It carries the seeds of plants, it guides the clouds, and it shapes the mountains. The elements are all connected, and if one is disrupted, the others will be affected. We must work together to protect the balance."

Zephyr's eyes softened, but he remained cautious. "You speak of interconnectedness, Raijin, but the wind is my domain. I have no desire to involve myself in the conflicts of the other elements. The sky is vast and free, and I intend to keep it that way."

Raijin realized that words alone would not convince Zephyr. He needed to show him the reality of the interconnectedness of the elements, to demonstrate how the balance of the world depended on their cooperation.

With a deep breath, Raijin raised the Sacred Hammer, summoning the power of the storm. The sky above darkened as storm clouds gathered, and the wind began to howl with increasing intensity. The once-gentle breeze turned into a powerful gale, and the air was filled with the roar of the storm.

Zephyr watched in surprise as the once-calm sky was transformed into a chaotic tempest. The wind howled and whipped through the air, carrying with it the scent of rain and the sound of thunder. The clouds darkened, and the sky was filled with the crackle of lightning.

"Zephyr, this is the reality of the world," Raijin called out, his voice barely audible over the roar of the storm. "The elements are interconnected, and when one is disrupted, the others are affected. We must work together to restore the balance, or the world will be consumed by chaos."

Zephyr looked out at the raging storm, his expression one of deep contemplation. He could see the truth in Raijin's words—the wind, once free and playful, had been thrown into turmoil by the forces of the storm. The sky, once under his control, was now at the mercy of the thunder and lightning.

With a determined look, Zephyr raised his hands, summoning the power of the wind. The gale began to calm, and the storm gradually subsided. The clouds parted, and the sky was once again clear and blue.

Zephyr turned to Raijin, his eyes filled with a newfound understanding. "You are right, Raijin. The elements are interconnected, and we must work together to maintain the balance of the world. I see now that the wind cannot remain isolated from the other elements. We must cooperate to protect the natural order."

Raijin nodded, feeling a sense of relief as Zephyr stepped forward, extending his hand in a gesture of unity. "Thank you, Zephyr. The world needs us to work together, not against each other. Only then can we restore the balance and protect the natural order."

With Zephyr's agreement, the final battle was won. Raijin had faced each of the elemental deities, and through their cooperation, the balance of the world had been restored. The elements, once in conflict, were now in harmony, working together to protect the natural order.

The Wisdom of Cooperation

As Raijin returned to the heavenly realm, he felt a deep sense of fulfillment. The battles with the elemental deities had taught him invaluable lessons about the importance of cooperation and unity. He had seen firsthand how the elements were interconnected, and how their harmony was essential for the balance of the world.

Raijin knew that true power did not come from domination or control, but from working together with others to achieve a common goal. The elements, when united, were capable of incredible feats, and their combined strength was greater than any one force alone.

The Sacred Hammer, which had amplified Raijin's powers, was a symbol of this unity. It was a reminder that the elements were not separate, but part of a greater whole. The hammer's power came not from the weapon itself, but from the cooperation and harmony of the elements that it represented.

As Raijin stood at the edge of the heavenly realm, looking out over the world below, he felt a renewed sense of purpose. He knew that his journey was far from over, but he also knew that he had taken an important step toward fulfilling his destiny. With the lessons he had learned and the strength of his allies, Raijin was ready to face whatever challenges lay ahead.

The world was vast and full of mysteries, but Raijin knew that as long as the elements remained united, they could overcome any obstacle and protect the balance of the natural order. The power of unity and cooperation was the key to achieving harmony, and Raijin was determined to uphold that principle in all that he did.

With a final glance at the sky, Raijin turned and began his journey back to the heavenly realm, the wisdom of cooperation and the power of the elements etched into his heart and mind. He knew that the world depended on him and the other elemental deities, and together, they would ensure that the balance of the world was preserved for all time.

Chapter 7: The Temptation of Power

A Moment of Reflection

Raijin, the Thunder God, had faced many trials and battles on his journey to protect the balance of the world. He had overcome the elemental deities, forged alliances, and even claimed the Sacred Hammer, a powerful artifact that amplified his abilities. His journey had taught him invaluable lessons about cooperation, balance, and the true nature of power. Yet, as he stood on the precipice of his next challenge, he felt an uneasy stirring deep within his heart—a sense of foreboding that he could not ignore.

The world was vast and full of mysteries, and Raijin knew that his journey was far from over. But the trials he had faced so far had tested him in ways he had never imagined, pushing him to the limits of his strength, wisdom, and resolve. With each victory, he had grown stronger, but he had also become more aware of the immense responsibility that came with his power. The balance of the world was a delicate thing, and it was his duty to protect it, no matter the cost.

As Raijin stood at the edge of a towering cliff, gazing out over the endless expanse of the world below, he felt a deep sense of weariness. The battles he had fought had taken their toll, and he could feel the weight of his responsibilities pressing down on him like a heavy burden. He knew that the road ahead would be long and difficult, and he wondered if he had the strength to continue.

It was in this moment of vulnerability that a shadow fell over Raijin, and he felt the air around him grow cold. The sky, once clear and bright, darkened with ominous clouds, and the wind began to howl with a chilling intensity. Raijin turned, his senses on high alert, and saw a figure emerging from the shadows—a being unlike any he had encountered before.

The figure was tall and imposing, its form shrouded in darkness. Its eyes glowed with an eerie light, and its presence exuded a malevolent energy that made the hairs on the back of Raijin's neck stand on end. This was no ordinary creature—it was a dark spirit, a being that embodied greed, corruption, and the darker aspects of power.

The spirit's voice was a whisper on the wind, soft and seductive, yet filled with an underlying menace. "Raijin, Thunder God," it said, its tone almost mocking. "You have come far on your journey, and you have gained much power. But tell me, are you satisfied with what you have achieved? Or do you hunger for more?"

Raijin narrowed his eyes, sensing the danger in the spirit's words. "Who are you?" he demanded, his voice steady despite the unease he felt. "What do you want?"

The spirit's lips curled into a sinister smile. "I am but a humble servant of power," it replied, its voice smooth as silk. "I have come to offer you a gift—a gift of unlimited power, far beyond anything you have ever known. With it, you could achieve anything you desire, bend the world to your will, and become a god among gods."

Raijin felt a chill run down his spine at the spirit's words. The offer was tempting, undeniably so. The idea of unlimited power, of being able to shape the world as he saw fit, was a seductive one. But he also knew that there was a price to be paid for such power—a price that could cost him everything he held dear.

"I have no need for your gift," Raijin said firmly, his resolve unshaken. "I am the Thunder God, and I will protect the balance of the world with the power I have been given. I will not be swayed by greed or ambition."

The spirit's smile widened, its eyes glowing with a malevolent light. "Ah, but are you so certain? Power is a dangerous thing, Raijin, and it can be so easy to lose oneself in its embrace. You have already tasted power, have you not? The Sacred Hammer, the alliances you have forged, the battles you have won—all of these have given you a taste of what true power feels like. But it is only a taste. Imagine what you could achieve with the power I offer."

Raijin felt a flicker of doubt in his heart, a small crack in his resolve. The spirit's words were like a poison, seeping into his mind and feeding on his insecurities. He had indeed tasted power, and it had been exhilarating. The victories he had won, the respect he had earned—these were things that had fueled his desire to protect the world. But was it enough? Could he truly protect the balance of the world with the power he had, or was there more he needed to achieve his goal?

The spirit seemed to sense Raijin's hesitation, and it pressed its advantage. "Think of all you could do with unlimited power, Raijin," it whispered, its voice dripping with temptation. "You could end all conflict, bring peace to the world, and rule as a benevolent god. You could reshape the very fabric of reality, bend the elements to your will, and create a paradise where no one would dare to challenge you."

Raijin closed his eyes, trying to shut out the spirit's voice. But the temptation was strong, and he could feel the allure of the power being offered to him. He had always believed in the importance of balance, of using his power to protect rather than dominate. But what if he was wrong? What if the only way to truly protect the world was to wield absolute power, to impose order through sheer force?

As these thoughts swirled in Raijin's mind, he felt the spirit's presence growing stronger, its darkness wrapping around him like a suffocating shroud. The air grew colder, and the wind howled with a malevolent fury. The spirit's voice was relentless, a constant whisper in his ear, urging him to accept the power being offered.

"You know it to be true, Raijin," the spirit whispered. "Power is the only way to achieve your goals. Without it, you are nothing. With it, you could be everything."

Raijin's heart raced, his mind a battlefield of conflicting thoughts and emotions. He could feel the pull of the power, the temptation to give in and accept the spirit's offer. But deep within him, a voice of reason called out, reminding him of the values he held dear—the importance of balance, the need for cooperation, and the dangers of unchecked ambition.

Raijin knew that the power being offered to him was not a gift—it was a curse. It was a power that came at the cost of his morals, his integrity, and everything he stood for. To accept it would be to lose himself, to become something he had sworn never to be—a tyrant, consumed by greed and corruption.

With a surge of willpower, Raijin pushed back against the spirit's influence, his resolve hardening like steel. He opened his eyes, his gaze fierce and unwavering as he met the spirit's malevolent stare.

"I will not be swayed by your temptations," Raijin declared, his voice filled with conviction. "True power does not come from domination or control. It comes from staying true to one's values, from protecting those who cannot protect themselves, and from maintaining the balance of the world. I will not sacrifice my morals for the sake of power."

The spirit's smile faltered, its eyes narrowing with anger. "Foolish god," it hissed, its voice filled with venom. "You would throw away the chance to become the most powerful being in existence? You would reject the gift of unlimited power, all for the sake of your so-called morals?"

"Yes," Raijin replied without hesitation. "Power without integrity is meaningless. I will not be corrupted by greed or ambition, no matter how tempting the offer."

The spirit's eyes blazed with fury, its form writhing with dark energy. "You will regret this decision, Raijin," it snarled, its voice filled with malice. "I offer you one last chance—accept my gift, or face the consequences."

Raijin stood tall, his grip tightening on the Sacred Hammer. "I will not be swayed," he said firmly. "I choose righteousness over power, integrity over greed. If there are consequences to my decision, I will face them with my head held high."

With a roar of anger, the spirit lashed out, its dark energy surging toward Raijin like a tidal wave. But Raijin was ready. He raised the Sacred Hammer, summoning the power of the storm, and unleashed a bolt of lightning that shattered the spirit's attack.

The dark energy dissipated, and the spirit recoiled, its form flickering as if it were struggling to maintain its shape. Raijin could see the malevolence in its eyes, the burning hatred for those who refused to succumb to its temptations.

"You will pay for your defiance," the spirit spat, its voice dripping with venom. "You may have won this battle, but the war is far from over. Power is a seductive force, Raijin, and it will continue to haunt you, tempting you at every turn. One day, you will fall, just as others have before you."

With those final words, the spirit's form dissolved into the shadows, leaving behind a lingering sense of unease in the air. Raijin stood in silence, his heart still pounding from the encounter. He knew that the spirit's words were not entirely false—power was indeed a seductive force, and it would continue to test him throughout his journey.

But Raijin also knew that he had made the right choice. He had chosen to stay true to his values, to reject the corrupting influence of greed and ambition.

The temptation of power was strong, but his resolve was stronger. He would not allow himself to be swayed by darkness, no matter how alluring the offer.

The Story of the Fallen God

As Raijin continued his journey, he found himself reflecting on the encounter with the dark spirit. The temptation of power had been a harsh reminder of the dangers that came with his responsibilities as the Thunder God. He knew that he needed to remain vigilant, to guard against the corruption that could so easily take hold of those who wielded great power.

It was during one of these moments of reflection that Raijin remembered an ancient tale, a story passed down through the ages as a warning to all gods and mortals alike. It was the story of a fallen god, a once-noble deity who had been corrupted by the very power he sought to wield.

Long ago, in a time when the world was still young, there was a god known as Hikari, the Bringer of Light. Hikari was revered for his wisdom and compassion, and he was beloved by all who knew him. He had the power to illuminate even the darkest corners of the world, bringing hope and joy to all who basked in his light.

But as the years passed, Hikari began to grow restless. He saw the suffering and conflict in the world, and he longed to bring an end to it. He believed that with enough power, he could create a perfect world, a paradise where there would be no pain, no sorrow, and no darkness.

Driven by this desire, Hikari sought out a powerful artifact known as the Celestial Crown, a relic said to grant its wearer the power of the stars themselves. The crown was hidden deep within the heart of the cosmos, guarded by the ancient spirits of the universe. But Hikari, determined to achieve his vision, overcame the trials set before him and claimed the crown as his own.

With the Celestial Crown upon his head, Hikari's power grew exponentially. He could control the very fabric of reality, bend the laws of nature to his will, and reshape the world as he saw fit. But with this newfound power came a change in Hikari's heart. The once-noble god, who had sought to bring light to the world, began to see himself as a god above all others, a ruler who could impose his will on all creation.

Hikari's ambition grew, and he began to believe that only he could create the perfect world. He imposed his vision upon the world, erasing anything that did not fit his idea of perfection. Those who opposed him were cast into darkness, their voices silenced, their existence erased. The light that had once brought hope now became a tool of oppression, and the world began to wither under Hikari's rule.

The other gods, seeing the corruption that had taken hold of Hikari, tried to reason with him. They pleaded with him to remove the Celestial Crown, to return to the god he once was. But Hikari, consumed by his power, refused to listen. He saw the other gods as threats to his perfect world, and he turned against them, waging war against those who had once been his allies.

The battle that followed was cataclysmic, shaking the very foundations of the universe. The gods fought with all their might, but Hikari's power was overwhelming. One by one, the gods fell, their light extinguished by the god who had once been their friend.

But as the war raged on, Hikari began to realize the cost of his ambition. The world he had sought to protect was now a wasteland, its beauty marred by the scars of battle. The people he had sought to save now lived in fear, their joy replaced by despair. The light that had once guided him had become a source of darkness, consuming everything in its path.

In the end, Hikari's own creation turned against him. The Celestial Crown, sensing the corruption in Hikari's heart, rejected him, stripping him of his power and casting him into the void. The fallen god was left to wander the darkness, a shadow of his former self, forever tormented by the consequences of his unchecked ambition.

The story of Hikari served as a cautionary tale for all who sought power. It was a reminder that even the noblest of intentions could be twisted by greed and ambition, and that true power came not from domination, but from humility and integrity.

Raijin took the story to heart, vowing to never follow in Hikari's footsteps. He knew that the temptation of power was a dangerous thing, and that he must always remain vigilant against the darkness that lurked within. The encounter with the dark spirit had been a test, but it had also been a lesson—a lesson that he would carry with him for the rest of his journey.

The Power of Righteousness

As Raijin continued his journey, he found himself growing stronger, not just in his abilities, but in his resolve. The temptation of power had been a turning point, a moment of clarity that had reaffirmed his commitment to his values. He knew that true power did not come from the ability to dominate or control, but from the strength to stay true to oneself, even in the face of overwhelming temptation.

The road ahead was still fraught with challenges, but Raijin felt a renewed sense of purpose. He knew that his journey was far from over, and that there would be more tests of his strength, wisdom, and integrity. But he also knew that as long as he remained true to his values, he would be able to overcome any obstacle that stood in his way.

As he traveled, Raijin encountered many who sought his help—villages threatened by natural disasters, forests in need of protection, and people struggling to find their place in the world. Each time, he used his power not to impose his will, but to guide and protect, to help others find their own strength and to restore balance where it had been lost.

The lessons he had learned from the elemental deities, from the Sacred Hammer, and from the dark spirit all came together to shape the way Raijin wielded his power. He understood now that power was not something to be hoarded or flaunted, but something to be used with care and responsibility. It was a gift that came with great responsibility, and it was his duty to use it wisely.

The story of Hikari served as a constant reminder of the dangers of unchecked ambition, and Raijin made a conscious effort to remain humble, to seek the counsel of others, and to stay grounded in his values. He knew that the path of righteousness was not always easy, but it was the only path that would lead to true peace and harmony.

As Raijin stood on the edge of a cliff, looking out over the world he had sworn to protect, he felt a deep sense of peace. The journey ahead was still uncertain, but he was no longer afraid. He had faced the temptation of power and emerged stronger for it, his resolve unshaken and his heart filled with the knowledge that he was on the right path.

The world was vast and full of mysteries, but Raijin knew that as long as he remained true to his values, he would be able to navigate whatever challenges came his way. The power he wielded was not just a tool, but a reflection of who he was—a god who had chosen righteousness over greed, integrity over corruption, and balance over chaos.

With a final glance at the sky, Raijin turned and began his journey once more, the lessons of his past guiding him toward the future. The temptation of power was a challenge he would face again and again, but he knew that as long as he stayed true to himself, he would never fall into the darkness that had claimed so many before him.

He was the Thunder God, a protector of the balance, and he would continue to uphold the values that defined him. The world depended on him, and he was determined to fulfill his destiny, not through domination or control, but through righteousness, humility, and the unwavering commitment to doing what was right.

Chapter 8: The Alliance of the Beasts

A World in Peril

The world that Raijin, the Thunder God, had sworn to protect was vast and full of wonder, but it was also a place of great danger. As he continued his journey to maintain the balance of the natural order, he encountered news of a new and formidable threat—one that not only endangered the lands of mortals and gods alike, but also threatened the very existence of the mythical beasts that roamed the world.

This enemy was not like those Raijin had faced before. It was a force of unnatural power, a dark presence that sought to corrupt the world, bending it to its will. It spread like a blight, turning lush forests into barren wastelands, drying up rivers, and darkening the skies with clouds of malevolent energy. Wherever it went, life was extinguished, and the world grew colder, darker, and more desolate.

The mortal realms were in a state of panic, their rulers calling upon the gods for aid. But the gods, too, were troubled, sensing that this threat was not something that could be easily vanquished by divine power alone. This enemy was a force that fed on fear and chaos, growing stronger with every act of destruction it caused. It was a menace that needed to be confronted with more than just brute strength—it required unity, cooperation, and a deep understanding of the natural order.

Raijin knew that he could not face this enemy alone. The power of the storm was formidable, but it was only one part of the world's elemental forces. He needed allies—beings of immense power and wisdom who could help him in this battle. But these allies would not be gods or mortals; they would be the mythical beasts that roamed the ancient world, creatures of legend who had existed since the dawn of time.

The mythical beasts were known to be creatures of immense strength, intelligence, and power. They were beings of the natural world, deeply connected to the elements and the forces that governed the earth, sky, and sea. But they were also proud and independent, often choosing to remain hidden from the world, only revealing themselves in times of great need.

Raijin knew that forming an alliance with these legendary beasts would not be easy. It would require more than just a show of strength; it would require trust, respect, and a shared understanding of the importance of balance. He would need to earn their trust, forge bonds of friendship, and convince them that the threat they faced was one that could only be defeated through unity.

With a deep breath, Raijin set out on a journey to find the mythical beasts and to form an alliance that would protect their world from the looming darkness.

The Ancient Pact

Raijin's first destination was the sacred grove of the ancient druids, a place of deep magic and wisdom where the gods and mythical beasts had once made an ancient pact. The grove was a hidden sanctuary, protected by powerful wards and guarded by spirits of nature. It was a place where the veil between the mortal world and the realm of the beasts was thin, and where the old laws of cooperation and mutual respect still held sway.

As Raijin approached the grove, he could feel the ancient magic in the air. The trees were tall and majestic, their leaves shimmering with a soft, golden light. The ground was covered in a thick carpet of moss and flowers, and the air was filled with the sweet scent of blooming plants. It was a place of peace and tranquility, untouched by the blight that had spread across the world.

In the center of the grove stood a massive stone altar, covered in runes and symbols that glowed with an otherworldly light. This was the altar where the ancient pact had been made—a pact between the gods and the mythical beasts, forged in a time of great peril. The pact was a promise of mutual respect and cooperation, a vow to protect the balance of the world and to come to each other's aid in times of need.

Raijin approached the altar, his heart filled with reverence for the ancient pact. He knew that to earn the trust of the mythical beasts, he would need to honor this pact and uphold the values it represented. He knelt before the altar, placing his hand on the cold stone, and called out to the spirits of the grove.

"Spirits of the ancient grove, guardians of the old laws, I come before you as Raijin, the Thunder God," he said, his voice steady and clear. "I seek the aid of the mythical beasts, for the world is in great danger. The balance of nature is threatened, and only through unity and cooperation can we hope to protect it. I ask for your guidance and your blessing as I seek to honor the ancient pact."

For a moment, there was only silence, the grove filled with the gentle rustling of leaves and the soft hum of magic. But then, the air around the altar began to shimmer, and the runes on the stone glowed brighter. The spirits of the grove had heard Raijin's plea, and they were answering his call.

The shimmering air coalesced into a figure—a spirit of the grove, its form ethereal and graceful, made of light and shadow. The spirit's eyes were deep and wise, filled with the knowledge of ages past.

"Raijin, Thunder God," the spirit said, its voice like the whisper of the wind through the trees. "You come before us with a request that is both noble and necessary. The world is indeed in great danger, and the time has come for the ancient pact to be honored once more. But know this—trust is not easily earned, and the mythical beasts are proud and wary. You must prove yourself worthy of their alliance."

Raijin nodded, understanding the weight of the spirit's words. "I will do whatever it takes to earn their trust," he said with determination. "I seek not to command them, but to stand with them as equals, to protect the world we all hold dear."

The spirit regarded Raijin with a thoughtful gaze, then nodded slowly. "Very well," it said. "The path before you is fraught with challenges, but it is one you must walk with honor and courage. Go now, Raijin, and seek out the mythical beasts. Show them that you are true to your word, and that you are a worthy ally in the battle to come."

With that, the spirit faded away, leaving Raijin alone in the grove. But Raijin knew that he was not truly alone—the spirits of the grove had given him their blessing, and the ancient pact was now his to uphold. He rose to his feet, feeling a renewed sense of purpose, and set out to find the mythical beasts who would become his allies in the fight against the darkness.

The Griffin's Roar

Raijin's first destination was the high mountains of the north, where the griffins made their nests among the craggy peaks and towering cliffs. The griffins were legendary creatures, known for their strength, speed, and keen intellect. They were creatures of the sky, able to soar to great heights and strike with the ferocity of a storm. But they were also proud and fiercely independent, known to trust few and ally with even fewer.

As Raijin climbed the steep mountain paths, he could feel the cold wind biting at his skin, the air growing thinner with each step. The peaks loomed high above him, their jagged edges cutting into the sky like the claws of a great beast. It was a harsh and unforgiving land, but it was also a place of great beauty, where the forces of nature reigned supreme.

At the summit of the highest peak, Raijin found the nesting grounds of the griffins. The nests were large and made of twisted branches, bones, and the feathers of the griffins themselves. The creatures were perched on the edges of the cliffs, their golden eyes watching Raijin's approach with a mixture of curiosity and suspicion.

The largest of the griffins, a majestic creature with golden feathers and sharp, piercing eyes, stepped forward, its powerful wings flaring as it regarded Raijin with a wary gaze. This was the leader of the griffins, a creature of immense power and authority.

"Raijin, Thunder God," the griffin leader said, its voice a deep, resonant growl. "What brings you to our domain? The griffins have no need for gods or their conflicts. We are the masters of the sky, and we answer to no one."

Raijin bowed his head in respect, understanding the griffins' pride and independence. "I come not to command, but to ask for your help," he said. "The world is in great danger, and a darkness threatens to consume everything we hold dear. I seek to form an alliance with the mythical beasts, for together we can stand against this threat and protect the balance of the world."

The griffin leader tilted its head, its golden eyes narrowing as it considered Raijin's words. "An alliance?" it echoed, its tone skeptical. "And what makes you think the griffins would ally themselves with a god, even one as powerful as the Thunder God?"

Raijin met the griffin's gaze with unwavering resolve. "Because the threat we face is not one that can be defeated by strength alone," he said. "It is a force that feeds on fear and chaos, and it seeks to corrupt the very fabric of nature. If we do not stand together, we will all fall, one by one, until there is nothing left. But if we unite, if we trust in each other's strength and wisdom, we can overcome this darkness and protect the world we love."

The griffin leader was silent for a long moment, its eyes studying Raijin with an intensity that made him feel as if the creature was peering into his very soul. Then, slowly, the griffin nodded, a low rumble of approval emanating from its throat.

"You speak with wisdom and conviction, Raijin," the griffin leader said. "And you are right—this is not a battle we can fight alone. The griffins will stand with you, Thunder God, and we will lend you our strength in the fight to come. But know this—we do not take this alliance lightly. You have earned our trust today, but trust must be maintained. If you betray us, if you fail to honor the pact, you will find that the wrath of the griffins is not something to be trifled with."

Raijin bowed deeply, his heart filled with gratitude and respect for the griffins. "I understand, and I will honor the pact with all my strength," he said. "Together, we will protect the balance of the world."

With the griffins' alliance secured, Raijin knew that his next task was to find other mythical beasts who could aid in the battle to come. The journey was far from over, but the bond he had forged with the griffins was a promising start.

The Dragon's Flame

Leaving the mountains behind, Raijin traveled to the volcanic regions of the south, where the dragons made their lairs deep within the fiery caverns and molten rivers. The dragons were among the most powerful and ancient of the mythical beasts, creatures of immense strength, wisdom, and fiery breath that could melt stone and steel alike. They were beings of the earth and fire, deeply connected to the primal forces that shaped the world.

The journey to the dragons' domain was perilous, the air thick with the scent of sulfur and the ground trembling with the constant rumbling of the volcanoes. Rivers of molten lava flowed through the landscape, their bright orange glow casting eerie shadows on the jagged rocks. The heat was intense, the air itself seeming to shimmer with the power of the flames.

As Raijin approached the entrance to the largest volcano, he could feel the ground shake beneath his feet, a deep growl resonating from within the earth. The entrance to the dragons' lair was a massive cavern, its walls lined with glowing crystals and ancient carvings depicting the dragons' history and their connection to the forces of nature.

Inside the cavern, Raijin found himself surrounded by the dragons. Their massive forms filled the space, their scales shimmering with shades of red, gold, and black. Their eyes glowed like molten embers, and their breaths filled the air with the scent of fire and smoke. The heat was almost unbearable, but Raijin stood his ground, knowing that he was in the presence of some of the most powerful beings in existence.

The largest of the dragons, a massive creature with scales as black as obsidian and eyes that burned like the heart of a volcano, stepped forward. This was the Dragon King, the ruler of the dragons and the keeper of the ancient flames.

"Raijin, Thunder God," the Dragon King rumbled, its voice deep and resonant, like the rumble of a distant earthquake. "You stand before the dragons, the ancient keepers of the earth's fire. What is it that you seek in our domain?"

Raijin bowed deeply, showing his respect for the Dragon King and the other dragons. "I come seeking an alliance," he said. "A darkness has spread across the world, threatening to consume all that we hold dear. This is a battle that cannot be won by gods or mortals alone. We need the strength and wisdom of the dragons to stand against this threat and protect the balance of nature."

The Dragon King's eyes narrowed, the flames within them flickering with a dangerous intensity. "An alliance with the dragons is not something to be taken lightly, Raijin," it said. "We are beings of immense power, and we have seen many gods come and go, each one seeking to wield our strength for their own purposes. Why should we trust you, Thunder God? What makes you worthy of our alliance?"

Raijin met the Dragon King's gaze with calm determination. "Because I seek not to command, but to stand as an equal," he said. "I understand the power of the dragons, and I respect the ancient wisdom you possess. But I also know that this is not a battle that can be won by strength alone. The darkness we face feeds on chaos and fear, and it seeks to corrupt the natural order. If we do not stand together, it will consume us all. But if we unite, if we trust in each other's strength and wisdom, we can protect the world and the balance that sustains it."

The Dragon King was silent for a long moment, its gaze never leaving Raijin's. The heat in the cavern seemed to intensify, the flames within the dragons' eyes burning brighter as they considered Raijin's words.

Finally, the Dragon King let out a low rumble of approval. "You speak with the wisdom of the ancients, Raijin," it said. "And you are right—this is not a battle we can fight alone. The dragons will stand with you, Thunder God, and we will lend you our flames in the fight to come. But know this—the dragons are not to be trifled with. Our alliance is forged in fire, and fire can both create and destroy. Honor the pact, and you will have our strength. Betray it, and you will feel the full fury of the dragons' wrath."

Raijin bowed deeply once more, his heart filled with gratitude and respect for the dragons. "I will honor the pact with all my strength," he said. "Together, we will protect the balance of the world."

With the dragons' alliance secured, Raijin knew that his next task was to find the final group of mythical beasts who could aid in the battle to come. The journey was nearing its end, but the bonds he had forged with the griffins and dragons gave him hope for the battle ahead.

The Phoenix's Rebirth

Raijin's final destination was the lush and vibrant forests of the east, where the phoenixes made their nests among the ancient trees and hidden groves. The phoenixes were legendary creatures of fire and rebirth, known for their ability to rise from their own ashes, renewed and more powerful than before. They were beings of life and renewal, deeply connected to the cycles of nature and the eternal dance of creation and destruction.

The journey to the phoenixes' domain was one of serenity and beauty, the forest filled with the sounds of birdsong and the scent of blooming flowers. The trees were ancient and majestic, their branches reaching high into the sky, creating a canopy of green and gold. The air was warm and fragrant, filled with the energy of life and renewal.

As Raijin walked through the forest, he felt a deep sense of peace and reverence for the natural world. The forest was a place of healing and growth, a sanctuary where the forces of life and death were in perfect balance. It was a place where the phoenixes, creatures of fire and rebirth, had chosen to make their home.

In the heart of the forest, Raijin found the nesting grounds of the phoenixes. The nests were made of golden branches and filled with soft, glowing embers. The phoenixes themselves were perched among the trees, their feathers shimmering with shades of red, orange, and gold. Their eyes were filled with the wisdom of ages, and their presence exuded a sense of calm and renewal.

The largest of the phoenixes, a magnificent creature with feathers that glowed like the setting sun and eyes that burned with the intensity of a thousand flames, stepped forward. This was the Phoenix Queen, the ruler of the phoenixes and the keeper of the eternal flame.

"Raijin, Thunder God," the Phoenix Queen said, her voice melodic and soothing, like the gentle crackle of a warm fire. "You stand before the phoenixes, the eternal beings of fire and rebirth. What is it that you seek in our domain?"

Raijin bowed deeply, showing his respect for the Phoenix Queen and the other phoenixes. "I come seeking an alliance," he said. "A darkness has spread across the world, threatening to extinguish the light of life and renewal. This is a battle that cannot be won by gods or mortals alone. We need the strength and wisdom of the phoenixes to stand against this threat and protect the balance of nature."

The Phoenix Queen regarded Raijin with a thoughtful gaze, her eyes glowing with the light of the eternal flame. "An alliance with the phoenixes is not something to be taken lightly, Raijin," she said. "We are beings of rebirth and renewal, and we have seen many cycles of life and death come and go. Why should we trust you, Thunder God? What makes you worthy of our alliance?"

Raijin met the Phoenix Queen's gaze with calm determination. "Because I seek not to command, but to stand as an equal," he said. "I understand the power of the phoenixes, and I respect the ancient wisdom you possess. But I also know that this is not a battle that can be won by strength alone. The darkness we face seeks to corrupt the natural order and extinguish the light of life. If we do not stand together, it will consume us all. But if we unite, if we trust in each other's strength and wisdom, we can protect the world and the balance that sustains it."

The Phoenix Queen was silent for a long moment, her gaze never leaving Raijin's. The warmth in the air seemed to intensify, the flames within the phoenixes' eyes burning brighter as they considered Raijin's words.

Finally, the Phoenix Queen let out a soft, melodic cry of approval. "You speak with the wisdom of the ancients, Raijin," she said. "And you are right—this is not a battle we can fight alone. The phoenixes will stand with you, Thunder God, and we will lend you our flames of rebirth in the fight to come. But know this—the phoenixes are beings of renewal, and our alliance is one of mutual respect and trust. Honor the pact, and you will have our strength. Betray it, and you will find that even the light of life can be extinguished."

Raijin bowed deeply once more, his heart filled with gratitude and respect for the phoenixes. "I will honor the pact with all my strength," he said. "Together, we will protect the balance of the world."

With the phoenixes' alliance secured, Raijin knew that his journey was complete. He had forged bonds of trust and friendship with the griffins, dragons, and phoenixes, and together they would stand against the darkness that threatened to consume the world.

The Alliance of the Beasts

With the alliances secured, Raijin returned to the sacred grove, where the spirits of the ancient druids had first guided him on his journey. The mythical beasts—the griffins, dragons, and phoenixes—accompanied him, their presence a testament to the bonds of trust and friendship that had been forged.

As they gathered around the stone altar, the air was filled with a sense of anticipation and determination. The mythical beasts, once proud and independent, now stood united with Raijin, ready to face the common enemy that threatened their world.

The spirit of the grove appeared once more, its form shimmering with light and shadow. It regarded Raijin and the mythical beasts with a gaze filled with pride and respect.

"Raijin, Thunder God," the spirit said, its voice filled with warmth. "You have done well. The ancient pact has been honored, and the bonds of trust and friendship have been forged anew. Together, you stand as a united force, ready to protect the balance of the world."

Raijin nodded, feeling a deep sense of fulfillment. "We will face the darkness together," he said. "As allies, as friends, and as protectors of the natural order."

The spirit smiled, its light growing brighter. "The strength of this alliance is not in the power of each individual, but in the unity and trust that binds you together. Remember this as you face the challenges ahead. The darkness is strong, but it is not invincible. Together, you have the power to overcome it and to protect the world for generations to come."

With those words, the spirit of the grove faded away, leaving Raijin and the mythical beasts to stand together, united in purpose and resolve. The battle ahead would be difficult, but they were ready to face it, knowing that their strength lay not just in their power, but in the bonds of friendship and trust that had been forged.

As the first rays of dawn broke through the trees, casting a golden light over the grove, Raijin and his new allies prepared to face the darkness that threatened their world. The alliance of the beasts was strong, and together they would protect the balance of the natural order, no matter the cost.

Chapter 9: The Shadow of Betrayal

A Time of Triumph

The world stood at the edge of a precipice. The darkness that had been spreading across the lands, turning lush forests into barren wastelands and poisoning the rivers, was more insidious than any force Raijin, the Thunder God, had ever encountered. But despite the overwhelming threat, there was hope. Raijin had formed alliances with powerful mythical beasts—the griffins, the dragons, and the phoenixes—uniting them under a single banner to protect the balance of the natural order. Together, they had faced the encroaching darkness with courage and determination.

The early battles had gone well. The combined might of Raijin and his allies had managed to push back the dark forces, reclaiming some of the lands that had fallen under its corrupting influence. Each victory brought renewed strength to their cause, and Raijin's resolve grew stronger with each step forward. The bond he shared with his allies was deep, built on mutual respect, trust, and the shared goal of preserving their world.

Raijin felt a deep sense of pride in what they had achieved together. He knew that the journey ahead would still be long and arduous, but with his allies by his side, he was confident that they could overcome any challenge. The strength of their unity was unparalleled, and for the first time since the darkness had descended upon the world, Raijin allowed himself to believe that they might actually succeed in driving it away.

But even as Raijin stood tall in the light of their victories, a shadow loomed on the horizon—a shadow that would soon cast a long and terrible darkness over their hard-won triumphs.

The Arrival of the Stranger

It was during a time of relative calm, as Raijin and his allies regrouped and prepared for their next battle, that a stranger arrived at their camp. The stranger appeared out of the mists of the early morning, emerging from the shadows as if materializing from the very air itself. His appearance was unassuming—a traveler dressed in simple robes, his face obscured by the hood that covered his head.

The stranger's arrival was noticed by one of the griffins, who was patrolling the perimeter of the camp. The griffin, sensing no immediate threat, escorted the stranger to Raijin's tent, where the Thunder God was meeting with the leaders of the allied forces. Raijin, ever vigilant but also open to the possibility of new allies, allowed the stranger to enter, curious to hear what he had to say.

The stranger bowed respectfully before Raijin and the assembled leaders. "My lord Raijin," he said in a voice that was soft and melodic, yet carried a strange undertone that made the hairs on the back of Raijin's neck stand on end. "I bring news from the far reaches of the land. I have traveled a great distance to find you, for I seek to offer my aid in your noble quest to drive back the darkness."

Raijin studied the stranger carefully, his instincts telling him to be cautious. There was something about the man's presence that unsettled him, though he could not quite place what it was. Nevertheless, Raijin chose to listen, for the fight against the darkness required every bit of strength and knowledge they could muster.

"What news do you bring?" Raijin asked, his voice calm and measured.

The stranger lifted his head slightly, revealing a pair of sharp, gleaming eyes beneath the shadow of his hood. "The darkness you fight is powerful, my lord, and it is growing stronger with each passing day. But there is a way to defeat it—a way that has been long forgotten by the world. I know of an ancient relic, hidden deep within the mountains, that holds the power to vanquish the darkness once and for all. With this relic in your possession, you will have the strength to turn the tide of battle and bring peace to the land."

Raijin's interest was piqued. The idea of an ancient relic with the power to destroy the darkness was tempting, and it was not uncommon for such powerful artifacts to be hidden away in the remote corners of the world. But Raijin's caution remained, and he knew that such promises often came with a price.

"Why do you come to me with this knowledge?" Raijin asked. "And how can I trust that what you say is true?"

The stranger's eyes glinted with a strange light. "I come to you because I believe in your cause, my lord. I have seen the devastation wrought by the darkness, and I wish to see it ended as much as you do. As for trust, I understand your caution, but I ask that you take this leap of faith. Allow me to guide you to the relic, and you will see for yourself the truth of my words."

Raijin was silent for a moment, weighing the stranger's words carefully. The idea of a relic that could turn the tide of the battle was alluring, but he knew better than to act on impulse. He glanced at his allies—the griffins, the dragons, and the phoenixes—all of whom watched the stranger with wary eyes. They, too, sensed that something was amiss, but like Raijin, they understood the importance of seizing any advantage they could in the fight against the darkness.

Finally, Raijin nodded. "Very well," he said. "You will guide us to this relic. But know this—I will not tolerate deceit. If your words prove false, you will answer for it."

The stranger bowed once more, his voice smooth as silk. "You have my word, my lord. I will lead you to the relic, and together we will end the darkness."

With that, the plan was set in motion. The stranger would lead Raijin and a select group of his most trusted allies to the location of the relic, while the rest of the allied forces remained behind to guard their camp and continue their preparations for the next battle.

As Raijin prepared to set out on the journey, a deep sense of unease settled in his chest. He could not shake the feeling that something was wrong, but the promise of the relic was too great to ignore. He reminded himself of the ancient wisdom that had guided him on his journey—the wisdom of caution and discernment in choosing allies. He would need to be vigilant, for the shadow of betrayal was closer than he realized.

The Journey to the Mountains

The journey to the mountains was long and arduous, the path winding through dense forests, treacherous ravines, and steep cliffs. The air grew colder as they ascended, the sky darkening with clouds that threatened to unleash a storm at any moment. Raijin led the way, with the stranger guiding them from just behind, his movements smooth and effortless as he navigated the rugged terrain.

Raijin's chosen companions for the journey included a griffin, a dragon, and a phoenix—three of his most trusted allies, each representing the strength and wisdom of their respective kin. The griffin, with its keen eyes and sharp talons, was ever watchful, scanning the horizon for any sign of danger. The dragon, with its fiery breath and unyielding courage, was a formidable force, ready to strike at a moment's notice. The phoenix, with its radiant feathers and power of renewal, brought a sense of hope and resilience to the group.

As they traveled, Raijin could not help but notice that the stranger seemed to know the path well, guiding them with confidence and ease. But the sense of unease in Raijin's heart only grew stronger with each step. The deeper they ventured into the mountains, the more isolated and vulnerable they became, and Raijin's instincts told him to remain on guard.

Finally, after several days of travel, the group reached the entrance to a hidden cave, nestled deep within the mountains. The cave was dark and foreboding, its entrance lined with jagged rocks that seemed to form a natural barrier against intruders. The air was thick with the scent of earth and stone, and a cold wind whispered through the narrow passage, carrying with it a sense of foreboding.

The stranger halted at the entrance, turning to face Raijin and his companions. "The relic lies within this cave," he said, his voice calm and steady. "But be warned—this place is ancient and filled with dangers. We must proceed with caution."

Raijin nodded, his grip tightening on the Sacred Hammer. "We will be careful," he said. "Lead the way."

The stranger stepped forward, and the group followed him into the darkness of the cave. The passage was narrow and winding, the walls closing in around them as they descended deeper into the earth. The only light came from the occasional glow of the phoenix's feathers, casting eerie shadows on the rough stone walls.

As they ventured deeper into the cave, Raijin's unease grew stronger. The air was thick with tension, and he could feel the presence of something ancient and powerful lurking in the shadows. The silence was oppressive, broken only by the sound of their footsteps echoing off the stone.

Finally, after what felt like an eternity, the passage opened up into a vast chamber, its ceiling lost in darkness. In the center of the chamber stood a massive stone pedestal, upon which rested an ancient relic—a staff made of blackened wood, its surface etched with glowing runes that pulsed with a dark energy.

Raijin approached the pedestal cautiously, his eyes fixed on the relic. There was something about it that unsettled him—a sense of malevolence that radiated from the staff like a dark aura. He could feel the power within it, but it was not the kind of power that brought light or hope. It was a power that whispered of corruption, of darkness that consumed everything in its path.

"This is the relic," the stranger said, his voice smooth and reassuring. "With this staff in your possession, you will have the strength to vanquish the darkness once and for all."

But Raijin hesitated, his instincts screaming at him to stop. There was something wrong—terribly wrong. He could feel it in his bones, in the way the air seemed to thicken with each passing moment. The relic was not a weapon of light, but a tool of darkness, a conduit for the very force they had been fighting against.

"No," Raijin said, his voice firm. "This is not what it seems. This staff is not a relic of light—it is a relic of the darkness. It is a trap."

The stranger's eyes glinted with a malevolent light, and his lips curled into a sinister smile. "Very perceptive, Thunder God," he said, his voice dripping with venom. "But it is too late. The trap has already been sprung."

The Betrayal Unveiled

As the stranger spoke, the air in the chamber seemed to shift, the darkness growing thicker and more oppressive. The relic on the pedestal pulsed with a sinister energy, and the runes on its surface glowed brighter, casting an eerie light that illuminated the chamber.

The stranger's form began to change, his body shifting and warping as if it were made of liquid shadow. His features became more grotesque, his limbs elongating, his eyes turning into dark, empty voids. The creature that now stood before Raijin and his allies was no longer a man, but a shape-shifter—a being of pure darkness and deception.

The shape-shifter let out a chilling laugh, its voice echoing off the stone walls of the chamber. "You were so easily deceived, Raijin," it sneered. "You and your precious allies. Did you really think you could stand against the darkness? Did you really think you could trust anyone in this world?"

Raijin's heart sank as the full realization of the betrayal hit him. The stranger—this creature of darkness—had led them into a trap, using their hope and desperation against them. And now, they were surrounded by the very force they had been fighting to destroy.

The shape-shifter raised its hands, and the darkness in the chamber began to coalesce, forming tendrils of shadow that snaked their way toward Raijin and his companions. The air was filled with the sound of hissing and whispering, as if the shadows themselves were alive, eager to consume their prey.

Raijin reacted quickly, raising the Sacred Hammer and summoning the power of the storm. Lightning crackled in the air, and thunder rumbled as he unleashed a powerful bolt of energy toward the shape-shifter. But the creature moved with unnatural speed, dodging the attack with ease and laughing as it did so.

The griffin, dragon, and phoenix sprang into action, their powerful forms filling the chamber as they prepared to fight. The griffin let out a mighty roar, its sharp talons slashing through the tendrils of shadow. The dragon unleashed a torrent of fire, the flames illuminating the darkness and burning away the encroaching shadows. The phoenix spread its wings, its radiant feathers glowing with a brilliant light that pushed back the darkness.

But the shape-shifter was relentless, its form shifting and changing as it attacked. It moved with the fluidity of a shadow, its body twisting and warping in ways that defied the laws of nature. The tendrils of shadow it commanded were like living creatures, slithering through the air and striking with deadly precision.

Despite their strength and courage, Raijin and his allies were quickly overwhelmed. The darkness was too strong, too pervasive, and it seemed to feed on their fear and despair. The chamber became a battleground of light and shadow, but the darkness was winning, inch by inch.

Raijin fought with all his might, his heart filled with determination to protect his allies and to drive back the darkness. But the betrayal had shaken him to his core, and the pain of that betrayal weighed heavily on his soul. He had trusted the wrong ally, and now they were all paying the price.

In the chaos of the battle, Raijin saw the shape-shifter slip through the shadows, making its way toward the relic on the pedestal. With a sinking feeling, Raijin realized what the creature was planning—it intended to use the staff to amplify its power, to unleash the full force of the darkness upon them.

"No!" Raijin shouted, rushing toward the pedestal with all the speed he could muster. But the shadows were closing in, and he could feel their cold touch dragging him down, sapping his strength.

The shape-shifter reached the pedestal, its twisted form wrapping around the staff as it prepared to claim its power. The chamber seemed to tremble with anticipation, the air crackling with dark energy as the creature prepared to unleash the final blow.

But just as the shape-shifter was about to grasp the staff, a blinding light filled the chamber. The light was so intense that it seemed to burn away the shadows, pushing back the darkness with a force that was both overwhelming and purifying.

Raijin looked up to see the phoenix, its radiant feathers glowing brighter than ever before. The creature had unleashed the full power of its light, sacrificing itself in a final act of defiance against the darkness.

The shape-shifter let out a scream of rage and pain as the light engulfed it, burning away its shadowy form and severing its connection to the staff. The darkness that had filled the chamber began to dissipate, retreating from the purifying light of the phoenix.

But the cost was great. The phoenix's light began to fade, its brilliant feathers turning to ash as its life force was consumed by the act of sacrifice. The griffin and dragon let out cries of grief as their ally fell, its once-magnificent form reduced to a pile of glowing embers.

Raijin felt a deep pain in his heart as he watched the phoenix's sacrifice. The betrayal had led to a devastating loss, and the consequences of that betrayal would be felt for a long time to come. The shape-shifter was defeated, but the cost had been too high.

The Pain of Loss

The chamber was silent, the echoes of the battle fading into the darkness. The relic on the pedestal remained untouched, its malevolent energy still pulsing, but its power had been neutralized by the phoenix's light. The shape-shifter was gone, its form burned away by the purifying fire, but the pain of betrayal and loss lingered in the air.

Raijin knelt beside the pile of embers that had once been the phoenix, his heart heavy with grief. The creature had been a loyal ally, a beacon of hope and renewal in the darkest of times, and its loss was a devastating blow. Raijin felt a deep sense of responsibility for what had happened—he had trusted the wrong ally, and that trust had led to the death of a friend.

The griffin and dragon stood beside Raijin, their eyes filled with sorrow and anger. They, too, had been betrayed, and the pain of that betrayal was etched into their hearts. The bond they shared with Raijin had been tested, and though they remained united in their cause, the shadow of doubt lingered in the air.

Raijin knew that they could not stay in the chamber any longer. The relic, though neutralized for now, was still a threat, and the darkness that had spread across the world was still out there, waiting for another opportunity to strike. They needed to return to their camp, to regroup and prepare for the battles that lay ahead.

But as they made their way out of the cave, the weight of the betrayal and the loss they had suffered hung heavily over them. The victory they had sought had been tainted by deceit, and the pain of that deceit would take time to heal.

The Wisdom of Caution

As they descended from the mountains and returned to their camp, Raijin found himself reflecting on the ancient wisdom that had guided him throughout his journey. The wisdom of caution, of discernment in choosing allies, had been a lesson he had learned many times, but never had it been so painfully clear as it was now.

Trust was a powerful thing, but it was also fragile. It could be easily given, but once broken, it was difficult to repair. Raijin knew that he had made a mistake in trusting the shape-shifter, but he also knew that he could not allow that mistake to define him. The pain of betrayal was sharp, but it was also a reminder of the importance of vigilance, of the need to be ever watchful and discerning in the battles to come.

Raijin gathered his allies—the griffins, the dragons, and the remaining mythical beasts—and shared with them the story of the betrayal. He spoke of the shape-shifter's deceit, of the pain of losing the phoenix, and of the importance of staying true to their cause, even in the face of such a devastating loss.

"We have been betrayed," Raijin said, his voice filled with a quiet strength. "But we cannot let that betrayal break us. We must be vigilant, we must be wise, and we must be strong. The darkness is still out there, and it will not rest until it has consumed everything we hold dear. But we will not let it win. We will stand together, and we will fight for the balance of the world."

The mythical beasts listened to Raijin's words, their eyes filled with a renewed sense of purpose. They had suffered a great loss, but they were not defeated. They would honor the phoenix's sacrifice by continuing the fight, by standing together in the face of the darkness, and by trusting in the strength of their bonds.

As the sun set on the horizon, casting a golden light over the camp, Raijin felt a deep sense of resolve. The shadow of betrayal had fallen over them, but they had risen from it stronger, more determined than ever to protect the world they loved.

The battle ahead would be difficult, and the pain of loss would remain with them, but Raijin knew that they had the strength to endure. They would rise again, and they would face the darkness with the full force of their unity and resolve.

The story of the betrayal would be a lesson they would carry with them, a reminder of the importance of caution, of discernment, and of the resilience needed to rise again after a fall. And with that wisdom, they would continue their journey, ready to face whatever challenges lay ahead.

Chapter 10: The Descent into the Underworld

A Call from the Shadows

The world above was in turmoil. The darkness that had been spreading across the land had not yet been fully vanquished, despite the alliances Raijin, the Thunder God, had forged with the mythical beasts. The betrayal by the shape-shifter had left a scar on Raijin's heart, and the loss of the phoenix had been a devastating blow. But even as the battles raged on and the world teetered on the brink of chaos, a new challenge presented itself—one that would test Raijin in ways he had never imagined.

The call came to Raijin in the dead of night, as he rested in the heart of his camp, surrounded by his allies. It was not a call that could be heard with the ears, but one that resonated deep within his soul—a whisper from the shadows, a plea from the depths of the underworld. It was a voice he recognized, a voice filled with sorrow and longing.

The voice belonged to the phoenix—the very creature that had sacrificed itself to save Raijin and his allies from the shape-shifter's trap. Though its physical form had been reduced to ashes, its spirit had endured, trapped in the underworld, unable to move on to the next cycle of life. The phoenix's soul was bound to the world of the living by the power of its sacrifice, and it could not rest until it was set free.

Raijin's heart ached as he listened to the phoenix's plea. The creature had given everything to protect them, and now it was suffering in the darkness of the underworld, unable to find peace. Raijin knew that he could not ignore this call, no matter how dangerous the journey might be. He owed it to the phoenix—to all those who had sacrificed for the greater good—to make this journey and to bring the lost soul back from the depths of the underworld.

He rose from his resting place, his mind already made up. This was not a mission he could entrust to anyone else. The underworld was a place of great peril, a realm where the living were not welcome, and where even the mightiest gods feared to tread. But Raijin's resolve was strong, and his love for his fallen ally was stronger still.

As he prepared for the journey, Raijin knew that this would be one of the most difficult trials he had ever faced. The underworld was a realm of shadows and despair, a place where the rules of the living world did not apply. But Raijin also knew that he could not turn back. The phoenix had given everything for him, and now it was his turn to make a sacrifice in return.

The Journey Begins

The entrance to the underworld was hidden deep within the heart of a desolate wasteland, a place where the ground was cracked and barren, and the sky was perpetually overcast with dark, roiling clouds. The air was thick with the scent of decay, and the only sounds that could be heard were the distant wails of lost souls, carried on the wind like a mournful dirge.

Raijin stood at the edge of the great chasm that marked the boundary between the world of the living and the realm of the dead. The chasm was wide and deep, its depths shrouded in darkness, and a cold, unearthly wind blew up from its depths, chilling Raijin to the bone. This was the place where the souls of the dead crossed over into the underworld, where they were judged and sent to their final resting place.

As he gazed into the abyss, Raijin felt a shiver of fear run down his spine. The underworld was a place of great power and mystery, a realm that was governed by ancient laws and guarded by fearsome beings. To venture into this place was to risk everything, to face the unknown with nothing but his strength and resolve to guide him.

But Raijin did not hesitate. With a deep breath, he stepped forward and began his descent into the chasm. The ground beneath his feet crumbled away, and he felt himself falling, plunging into the darkness below. The wind howled around him, and the world above faded away, replaced by the cold, unrelenting grip of the underworld.

The descent seemed to last an eternity, the darkness growing thicker and more oppressive with each passing moment. Raijin could feel the weight of the underworld pressing down on him, a heavy, suffocating presence that threatened to crush his spirit. But he pressed on, determined to reach the phoenix's soul and bring it back to the world of the living.

Finally, after what felt like an age, Raijin's feet touched solid ground. He had reached the shores of the River Styx, the boundary between the world of the living and the underworld proper. The river was wide and dark, its waters black as ink and filled with the whispers of lost souls. The air was cold and still, and a thick mist hung over the water, obscuring the far shore.

Raijin knew that the only way to cross the river was to seek the aid of the ferryman, Charon, the ancient guardian of the Styx. Charon was a being of great power, a servant of the underworld who ferried the souls of the dead across the river in his ancient boat. But Charon was also a being who demanded payment for his services, and Raijin knew that the price of passage would be steep.

As Raijin stood on the shore, the mists parted, and the ferryman's boat appeared, gliding silently across the water. Charon himself stood at the helm, a tall, skeletal figure draped in tattered robes, his face hidden beneath a hood. His eyes glowed with an eerie light, and his bony hands gripped the long oar that propelled the boat through the dark waters.

Charon brought the boat to a stop at the shore and fixed Raijin with his glowing gaze. "Who dares to cross into the realm of the dead?" Charon's voice was a hollow rasp, like the creaking of ancient bones. "What business do you have in this place, where the living are not welcome?"

Raijin met Charon's gaze without flinching. "I am Raijin, the Thunder God," he said, his voice steady and unwavering. "I have come to reclaim the soul of the phoenix, who was taken before its time. I seek passage across the Styx, that I may bring the lost soul back to the world of the living."

Charon's eyes narrowed, and a low, rumbling growl echoed from deep within his chest. "The phoenix's soul belongs to the underworld now, Thunder God. It is not for the living to reclaim what has been taken by death."

Raijin felt a surge of determination. "The phoenix sacrificed itself to save the world from darkness," he said. "Its soul deserves to be set free, to be reborn and continue the cycle of life. I am willing to pay whatever price is required to cross the river and complete my journey."

Charon was silent for a long moment, his glowing eyes boring into Raijin's soul. Finally, he spoke. "The price of passage is steep, Raijin. You must offer something of great value, something that cannot be easily replaced. Only then will I grant you passage across the Styx."

Raijin reached into his robe and withdrew a small, intricately carved pendant—a relic of his past, a symbol of his divine lineage. It was a token of great significance, a reminder of his connection to the gods and his place in the world of the living. It was not something he parted with lightly, but he knew that it was the only thing of value he could offer.

"This pendant represents my connection to the world of the living," Raijin said as he held out the pendant to Charon. "It is a symbol of my divine lineage, of the power I wield as the Thunder God. I offer it to you as payment for passage across the Styx."

Charon studied the pendant for a moment, his bony fingers closing around it. Then, with a slow nod, he tucked the pendant away in the folds of his robes. "Very well, Raijin," he said. "The price has been paid. You may cross the river."

Raijin stepped into the boat, and Charon pushed off from the shore, guiding the vessel across the dark waters of the Styx. The whispers of lost souls filled the air, and the mist swirled around them, obscuring the world beyond. Raijin remained silent, his mind focused on the task ahead. He knew that the journey was only just beginning, and that the trials of the underworld would test him in ways he had never before experienced.

As they approached the far shore, Raijin could see the outline of a massive gate, its iron bars twisted and gnarled, covered in rust and the remnants of ancient spells. Beyond the gate lay the underworld proper, a realm of darkness and despair where the souls of the dead were judged and sent to their final resting place.

The boat came to a stop at the shore, and Raijin stepped out onto the cold, hard ground. Charon pointed to the gate, his bony finger trembling slightly. "Beyond this gate lies the realm of the dead, Raijin," he said. "Once you pass through, there is no turning back. You will face trials that will test your resolve, and you will encounter beings of great power who will seek to bar your way. But if you are true of heart, if your love for the phoenix is strong, you may yet succeed."

Raijin nodded, his grip tightening on the Sacred Hammer. "Thank you, Charon," he said. "I will see this through to the end."

With that, Raijin approached the gate, his heart pounding in his chest. The iron bars loomed before him, a barrier between the living and the dead, a boundary that few dared to cross. But Raijin was determined, and with a deep breath, he pushed open the gate and stepped into the underworld.

The Guardians of the Underworld

The underworld was a realm of shadows and echoes, a place where time seemed to have no meaning and where the very air was thick with the weight of sorrow and despair. The ground beneath Raijin's feet was cold and barren, a lifeless expanse that stretched out as far as the eye could see. The sky above was dark and featureless, a void that swallowed all light and hope.

Raijin could feel the presence of the underworld's guardians—ancient beings of immense power who watched over the souls of the dead and ensured that the living did not interfere with the natural order. These guardians were not to be taken lightly, for they were bound by the laws of the underworld, and their duty was to protect the realm from intruders.

As Raijin ventured deeper into the underworld, the first of these guardians appeared before him. It was the Ferryman's companion, the three-headed hound known as Cerberus, the fearsome guardian of the gates of the underworld. Cerberus was a massive beast, its three heads snarling and snapping as it barred Raijin's path. Each head was covered in thick, black fur, and its eyes glowed with a fierce, unnatural light. The ground shook beneath its paws, and its growls reverberated through the air like the rumble of distant thunder.

Raijin stopped in his tracks, knowing that to face Cerberus head-on would be a challenge unlike any he had ever encountered. The hound was a creature of the underworld, bound by the laws of death, and its strength was unmatched in this realm. But Raijin also knew that there was more to Cerberus than mere brute force. The creature was intelligent, cunning, and deeply loyal to its duty as a guardian.

"Cerberus," Raijin called out, his voice steady and calm. "I am Raijin, the Thunder God, and I seek passage through the underworld. I have come to reclaim the soul of the phoenix, who was taken before its time. I do not seek to disrupt the natural order, but to restore it."

Cerberus growled, its three heads lowering as it regarded Raijin with suspicion. The hound's eyes glinted with a mix of curiosity and wariness, and it took a step forward, its massive paws leaving deep impressions in the ground.

"You are a god of the living world," one of Cerberus's heads snarled. "This is not your realm, Thunder God. The souls of the dead belong to the underworld, and it is our duty to ensure that they remain here."

Raijin met the hound's gaze without flinching. "The phoenix's soul is bound by the power of its sacrifice," he said. "It cannot rest until it is set free. I ask for your permission to pass through the underworld, to retrieve the phoenix's soul and restore the balance of the world."

The three heads of Cerberus growled in unison, and for a moment, Raijin feared that the hound would attack. But then, the middle head spoke, its voice calmer and more measured than the others.

"The phoenix is a creature of rebirth," it said. "Its cycle of life and death is unlike that of any other being. You speak of restoring balance, Thunder God, but are you prepared to make the sacrifices necessary to achieve that goal? Are you willing to face the consequences of your actions?"

Raijin's heart was heavy with the weight of the decision he had made, but he knew that there was no turning back. "I am prepared," he said. "I will do whatever it takes to bring the phoenix's soul back to the world of the living, even if it means facing the trials of the underworld."

Cerberus's three heads exchanged glances, and then, slowly, the hound lowered itself to the ground, its growls subsiding. "Very well, Thunder God," the middle head said. "You may pass. But know this—the path ahead is fraught with danger, and the guardians of the underworld will not make your journey easy. You will need all the strength and resolve you can muster to succeed."

Raijin nodded in gratitude, feeling a sense of relief wash over him. "Thank you, Cerberus," he said. "I will honor the laws of the underworld and complete my journey with respect and determination."

With that, Cerberus stepped aside, allowing Raijin to continue on his journey. The hound's presence lingered in the air, a reminder of the power and authority of the underworld's guardians. But Raijin knew that this was only the beginning, and that the trials ahead would test him in ways he could not yet imagine.

The Trials of the Underworld

As Raijin ventured deeper into the underworld, the landscape around him began to change. The barren, lifeless ground gave way to twisted, gnarled trees, their branches clawing at the sky like the fingers of the damned. The air grew colder, and the shadows deepened, as if the very essence of the underworld was closing in around him.

The next guardian Raijin encountered was a figure of great power and authority, a being who embodied the very laws of life and death. It was Thanatos, the ancient god of death, who stood as a sentinel at the crossroads of the underworld. Thanatos was tall and imposing, his form shrouded in dark, flowing robes that seemed to merge with the shadows around him. His face was pale and gaunt, his eyes cold and unfeeling, and in his hand, he held a scythe that gleamed with a sharp, deadly light.

Raijin knew that Thanatos was not a being to be trifled with. The god of death was bound by the ancient laws that governed the underworld, and his duty was to ensure that the souls of the dead were judged and sent to their final resting place. But Raijin also knew that Thanatos was not without compassion, and that there was a chance—however slim—that he could be persuaded to allow Raijin to continue his journey.

"Thanatos, god of death," Raijin said as he approached the figure. "I am Raijin, the Thunder God, and I seek passage through the underworld. I have come to reclaim the soul of the phoenix, who was taken before its time. I ask for your permission to continue my journey."

Thanatos regarded Raijin with cold, calculating eyes, his grip tightening on the scythe. "You speak of reclaiming a soul, Thunder God," he said, his voice a low, resonant rumble. "But the souls of the dead belong to the underworld. They are judged according to the laws that govern this realm, and once they have crossed the threshold, they cannot return to the world of the living."

Raijin met Thanatos's gaze with determination. "The phoenix is a creature of rebirth," he said. "Its soul is bound by the cycle of life and death, but it cannot complete that cycle until it is set free. I do not seek to disrupt the natural order, but to restore it. The phoenix's soul deserves to be reborn, to continue its journey in the world of the living."

Thanatos was silent for a long moment, his eyes narrowing as he considered Raijin's words. The air around them grew colder, the shadows lengthening as if in response to the god of death's presence.

Finally, Thanatos spoke. "The phoenix is indeed a unique creature," he said. "Its cycle of life and death is unlike that of any other being, and its sacrifice has bound it to the underworld in a way that defies the natural order. But you speak of restoration, Thunder God, and that is something I cannot ignore."

Thanatos lowered his scythe, his expression softening slightly. "I will allow you to continue your journey, Raijin," he said. "But know this—the path ahead is perilous, and the trials you will face will test your resolve to its limits. You will need to make sacrifices of your own if you are to succeed. Are you prepared for that?"

Raijin's heart was heavy with the weight of Thanatos's words, but he knew that there was no other choice. "I am prepared," he said. "I will do whatever it takes to bring the phoenix's soul back to the world of the living, even if it means making sacrifices of my own."

Thanatos nodded, a faint glimmer of respect in his cold eyes. "Very well, Thunder God," he said. "Continue on your journey, and may you find the strength to complete it."

With that, Thanatos stepped aside, allowing Raijin to continue on his path. The god of death's presence lingered in the air, a reminder of the gravity of the journey Raijin had undertaken. But Raijin knew that he could not turn back. The phoenix's soul was waiting for him, and he would not rest until he had fulfilled his promise.

The Realm of Souls

The final trial awaited Raijin in the heart of the underworld, where the souls of the dead were judged and sent to their final resting place. This was the realm of Hades, the ruler of the underworld, a place of shadows and echoes where the souls of the dead lingered, awaiting their fate.

As Raijin approached the great hall of judgment, he could feel the weight of the souls pressing down on him, their whispers filling the air like a chorus of despair. The ground beneath his feet was cold and unforgiving, and the air was thick with the scent of decay. The hall itself was a massive structure, its walls lined with the tormented faces of the damned, their eyes filled with eternal sorrow.

At the far end of the hall sat Hades, the lord of the underworld, his throne carved from the bones of the dead. Hades was a fearsome figure, his form draped in black robes that seemed to absorb the light around him. His eyes were cold and calculating, and in his hand, he held a staff topped with a skull, its empty eye sockets glowing with an eerie light.

Raijin knew that this was the final trial, the last barrier between him and the phoenix's soul. Hades was a being of immense power, a ruler who commanded the underworld with an iron fist. To face him was to face the very essence of death itself, and Raijin knew that he would need all of his strength and resolve to succeed.

"Hades, lord of the underworld," Raijin said as he approached the throne. "I am Raijin, the Thunder God, and I have come to reclaim the soul of the phoenix. It was taken before its time, bound by the power of its sacrifice, and it cannot rest until it is set free. I ask for your permission to release the phoenix's soul and return it to the world of the living."

Hades regarded Raijin with cold, unfeeling eyes, his grip tightening on the staff. "You are a god of the living world, Raijin," he said, his voice a low, resonant rumble. "This is not your realm, and the souls of the dead belong to the underworld. The phoenix's soul has been judged and sent to its final resting place. It is not for you to reclaim what has been taken by death."

Raijin's heart sank at Hades's words. The price was steep—too steep, perhaps—but he knew that he had no other choice. The phoenix had given everything to save him and his allies, and now it was his turn to make a sacrifice in return.

With a heavy heart, Raijin stepped forward and knelt before Hades. "I offer my own soul in exchange for the phoenix's," he said, his voice steady and unwavering. "Take my soul and release the phoenix's. Let it be reborn and continue its journey in the world of the living."

Hades regarded Raijin with a cold, calculating gaze, his expression unreadable. For a long moment, the hall was silent, the whispers of the dead fading into the background as the lord of the underworld considered the offer.

Finally, Hades nodded, a faint smile playing on his lips. "Very well, Thunder God," he said. "Your sacrifice is accepted. The phoenix's soul will be released, and it will be reborn in the world of the living. But know this—your soul will remain here, bound to the underworld for all eternity."

Raijin felt a deep sense of peace as he accepted the terms of the bargain. The phoenix would be free, and that was all that mattered. He had fulfilled his promise, and he was willing to pay the price.

But as Hades raised his staff to seal the bargain, a blinding light filled the hall, and the air was filled with the sound of a mighty roar. Raijin looked up to see the phoenix, its radiant feathers glowing with a brilliant light, standing before him. The creature's eyes were filled with love and gratitude, and its presence filled the hall with warmth and hope.

The phoenix spread its wings, and the light grew brighter, enveloping Raijin and Hades in its glow. The air crackled with energy, and Raijin felt a surge of power coursing through his veins. The phoenix's sacrifice had bound it to the underworld, but its love and loyalty had given it the strength to break free.

With a final, triumphant cry, the phoenix released a burst of light that filled the entire hall, banishing the shadows and breaking the chains that bound its soul. The light enveloped Raijin, lifting him up from the cold ground and filling him with a sense of renewal and hope.

When the light finally faded, Raijin found himself back at the entrance to the underworld, the chasm before him and the world of the living beyond. The phoenix was by his side, its radiant feathers shimmering in the light of the rising sun. The journey was complete, and the phoenix's soul was free.

The Power of Sacrifice

As Raijin and the phoenix returned to the world of the living, he felt a deep sense of fulfillment. The journey to the underworld had tested him in ways he had never imagined, but it had also taught him the true meaning of sacrifice, love, and redemption. The phoenix's soul had been reclaimed, and it would be reborn, continuing its cycle of life and death as it was meant to.

Raijin knew that the battles ahead would still be difficult, and that the darkness had not yet been fully vanquished. But the strength and resolve he had gained from his journey into the underworld gave him hope. The power of sacrifice, the lengths one would go for those they loved, and the knowledge of life, death, and the cyclical nature of existence—these were the lessons that would guide him in the trials to come.

As the phoenix spread its wings and took flight, soaring into the sky with a renewed sense of purpose, Raijin knew that he, too, had been reborn. The underworld had tested his soul, but he had emerged stronger, more determined than ever to protect the balance of the world.

The journey was far from over, but Raijin was ready to face whatever challenges lay ahead. The power of love and sacrifice would guide him, and with the phoenix by his side, he would continue to fight for the world they both cherished.

And so, with the sun rising on the horizon, Raijin set out on the next chapter of his journey, his heart filled with hope and determination, knowing that the power of sacrifice and the love of those who had gone before him would see him through to the end.

Chapter 11: The Trial of the Mind

A Moment of Calm Before the Storm

Raijin, the Thunder God, had faced countless external battles on his journey to restore balance to the world. He had fought alongside mythical beasts, ventured into the underworld, and reclaimed the soul of the phoenix. Each challenge had tested his strength, resolve, and courage. But as he stood on the precipice of his next trial, Raijin knew that this one would be different. This would not be a battle against a tangible enemy, but a confrontation with his own mind—a trial that would force him to face his deepest fears and insecurities.

The world around him had grown quieter in the aftermath of his return from the underworld. The darkness that had threatened to consume everything was still present, but its advance had been slowed, giving Raijin and his allies a brief moment of respite. It was during this moment of calm that Raijin began to feel a growing unease within himself—a sense of doubt and fear that gnawed at the edges of his consciousness.

These feelings were not new to Raijin. Throughout his journey, he had been haunted by moments of doubt, by questions about his own worthiness and the path he had chosen. But he had always pushed these thoughts aside, focusing instead on the battles at hand. Now, however, there were no external enemies to fight, no immediate threats to distract him from the turmoil within. The fears and doubts that he had buried deep inside were rising to the surface, demanding to be confronted.

Raijin knew that he could not ignore these feelings any longer. The journey he had undertaken had been one of both external and internal challenges, and he understood that to truly restore balance to the world, he would need to first restore balance within himself. This would be his greatest trial yet—a trial of the mind, where he would be forced to confront the darkest parts of his soul and emerge stronger on the other side.

With a deep breath, Raijin steeled himself for what lay ahead. He knew that this would not be a trial he could face with strength alone. It would require introspection, self-awareness, and a willingness to confront the fears and insecurities that had plagued him for so long. It would require him to face himself.

The Temple of Reflection

Raijin's journey to the trial of the mind began with a visit to an ancient temple, hidden deep within a dense forest. The temple, known as the Temple of Reflection, was a place of great power and wisdom, a sanctuary where those seeking enlightenment could confront their inner demons and gain a deeper understanding of themselves. The temple was said to be guarded by spirits of the mind, beings who could peer into the very soul of those who entered, revealing their deepest fears and insecurities.

The forest surrounding the temple was thick with ancient trees, their branches intertwining to form a natural canopy that blocked out much of the sunlight. The air was cool and damp, and the ground was covered in a thick carpet of moss and fallen leaves. The only sounds were the rustling of leaves in the wind and the distant calls of birds hidden among the trees.

As Raijin approached the temple, he felt a sense of unease settle over him. The temple itself was a massive structure, built from smooth, dark stone that seemed to absorb the light rather than reflect it. The entrance was a large, arched doorway, flanked by statues of ancient gods and spirits, their faces stern and unforgiving. The temple exuded an aura of mystery and power, and Raijin could feel the weight of its history pressing down on him.

He stood before the entrance, his heart heavy with the knowledge of what awaited him inside. This was not a battle he could fight with his hammer or his powers. It was a battle that would take place within his own mind, a confrontation with the fears and doubts that had haunted him for so long.

With a deep breath, Raijin stepped forward and entered the temple. The air inside was cool and still, and the walls were lined with ancient runes and symbols that seemed to pulse with a faint, otherworldly light. The passageway led deep into the heart of the temple, and as Raijin walked, he could feel the presence of the spirits watching him, their eyes following his every move.

At the end of the passageway, Raijin entered a large, circular chamber. The floor was covered in smooth, polished stone, and in the center of the chamber was a large, ornate mirror, its surface reflecting the dim light of the chamber.

The mirror was the focal point of the room, and Raijin knew that it was here that the trial would begin.

He approached the mirror, his reflection staring back at him with an intensity that made him uneasy. The mirror was no ordinary glass—it was a portal into the mind, a gateway that would allow Raijin to confront the fears and doubts that had plagued him for so long. The spirits of the temple had created this mirror as a tool for self-reflection, a means by which those who entered could face their inner demons and gain a deeper understanding of themselves.

Raijin stood before the mirror, his heart pounding in his chest. He knew that once he looked into the mirror, there would be no turning back. He would be forced to confront the darkest parts of his soul, to face the fears and insecurities that had held him back for so long. But he also knew that this was a necessary step in his journey. To restore balance to the world, he would first need to restore balance within himself.

With a deep breath, Raijin gazed into the mirror, allowing himself to be drawn into its depths.

The Illusions of Fear

As Raijin stared into the mirror, the world around him began to shift and change. The chamber faded away, replaced by a dark, swirling void that seemed to stretch on forever. The mirror itself dissolved into the darkness, leaving Raijin standing alone in the emptiness, surrounded by nothing but shadows.

But he was not alone for long. As Raijin stood in the void, figures began to materialize around him—dark, twisted shapes that seemed to emerge from the shadows themselves. These figures were not human, nor were they gods or beasts. They were something else entirely—creatures born from the darkest corners of Raijin's mind, manifestations of his deepest fears and insecurities.

The first of these creatures was a towering figure, its body covered in jagged, blackened armor. Its eyes glowed with a malevolent light, and its presence exuded an aura of overwhelming power and dominance. This creature represented Raijin's fear of failure, the fear that he was not strong enough to protect the world, that he would be defeated by the darkness and lose everything he held dear.

The second creature was smaller, but no less terrifying. It had the appearance of a shadowy wraith, its form constantly shifting and changing, never solidifying into a single shape. This creature represented Raijin's fear of uncertainty, the fear that he did not truly know the path he was on, that he was wandering blindly through the darkness with no clear direction or purpose.

The third creature was the most unsettling of all. It had no clear form, its body a mass of writhing shadows that seemed to pulse with a sickly light. This creature represented Raijin's fear of his own power, the fear that the very force he wielded could become a tool of destruction rather than protection, that he could lose control and become the very thing he sought to destroy.

As these creatures surrounded him, Raijin felt a wave of fear and doubt wash over him. These were not enemies he could defeat with brute force or skill. They were manifestations of his own mind, reflections of the fears and insecurities that had haunted him for so long. To defeat them, he would need to confront the very things he had been avoiding—his own doubts, his own weaknesses.

The first creature, the armored figure, stepped forward, its eyes glowing with a fierce, malevolent light. "You are not strong enough, Raijin," it hissed, its voice echoing through the void like the clash of swords. "You are a failure. You have always been a failure. No matter how hard you try, you will never be able to protect those you care about. You will always be too weak."

Raijin felt a surge of anger and fear rise within him, but he forced himself to remain calm. He knew that this creature was a manifestation of his own fear, and that to defeat it, he would need to confront that fear head-on.

"I am not a failure," Raijin said, his voice steady. "I have faced many challenges, and I have overcome them all. I have protected those I care about, and I will continue to do so. I may not be perfect, but I am not weak."

The creature snarled, its eyes narrowing. "You think you are strong, but you are not," it spat. "You have been lucky, nothing more. Your strength is an illusion, a lie you tell yourself to hide from the truth. The truth is that you are powerless against the darkness."

Raijin felt the weight of the creature's words pressing down on him, but he refused to give in. "I am not powerless," he said, his voice growing stronger. "I have faced the darkness before, and I will face it again. My strength comes not from my power alone, but from my determination, from the love and trust of those who stand by my side. I will not let fear control me."

The creature let out a roar of anger, but its form began to waver, the edges of its body dissolving into the darkness. Raijin could feel its power weakening, the hold it had on him loosening. With a final surge of will, Raijin struck out at the creature, shattering it into a thousand pieces that dissolved into the void.

But the victory was short-lived. The second creature, the wraith-like figure, stepped forward, its body shifting and changing as it approached. "You do not know where you are going," it whispered, its voice like the rustle of leaves in the wind. "You are lost, wandering blindly through the darkness. You think you have a purpose, but you do not. You are a fool, Raijin, and your path will lead you to ruin."

Raijin felt a pang of doubt at the creature's words. It was true that he had questioned his path many times, that he had wondered if he was truly doing the right thing. The uncertainty of his journey had weighed heavily on him, and there were moments when he had felt lost, unsure of the choices he had made.

But Raijin knew that he could not allow this doubt to consume him. "I may not have all the answers," he said, his voice filled with resolve. "But I know that I am on the right path. I have made mistakes, but I have learned from them. I am guided by my love for the world, by my desire to protect those who cannot protect themselves. I will not let uncertainty stop me."

The wraith let out a soft, mocking laugh. "You think you are guided by love, but you are guided by fear," it whispered. "Fear of failure, fear of the unknown. You are afraid, Raijin, and that fear will lead you to ruin."

Raijin shook his head, refusing to be swayed. "I am afraid," he admitted. "But I will not let that fear control me. I will face it, and I will overcome it. I will continue on my path, no matter where it leads."

The wraith hissed in frustration, its form flickering and wavering. Raijin could feel its power weakening, the hold it had on him loosening. With a final burst of determination, Raijin struck out at the creature, shattering it into a thousand pieces that dissolved into the void.

But the trial was not over yet. The third creature, the mass of writhing shadows, stepped forward, its body pulsing with a sickly light. "You fear your own power," it whispered, its voice like the hiss of a snake. "You know that the power you wield is dangerous, that it could consume you. You are afraid of what you could become, of the destruction you could unleash. You fear that you will lose control, that you will become the very thing you seek to destroy."

Raijin felt a cold chill run down his spine. This was the fear that had haunted him the most—the fear that the power he wielded could become a force of destruction, that he could lose control and cause harm to those he sought to protect. It was a fear that he had buried deep inside, but it had always been there, lurking in the shadows of his mind.

But Raijin knew that he could not allow this fear to control him. "My power is a tool," he said, his voice filled with resolve. "It is a part of me, but it does not define me. I am in control of my power, and I will use it to protect, not to destroy. I will not let fear dictate my actions."

The creature let out a low, sinister laugh. "You think you are in control, but you are not," it whispered. "Power is a dangerous thing, Raijin. It corrupts, it consumes. You cannot control it forever. One day, it will consume you, and you will become the very darkness you seek to destroy."

Raijin felt the weight of the creature's words pressing down on him, but he refused to give in. "I will not let that happen," he said, his voice growing stronger. "I will remain vigilant, I will remain true to myself. I will not allow my power to consume me. I will use it for good, to protect those I care about. I will not become the darkness."

The creature snarled in frustration, its form flickering and wavering. Raijin could feel its power weakening, the hold it had on him loosening. With a final surge of will, Raijin struck out at the creature, shattering it into a thousand pieces that dissolved into the void.

The trial of the mind was over. The creatures that had represented Raijin's fears and insecurities had been defeated, their hold on him broken. But Raijin knew that the battle had not been won by strength alone. It had been won by self-awareness, by the willingness to confront his fears and doubts and to overcome them.

The Wisdom of Reflection

As the last of the illusionary creatures dissolved into the void, the dark, swirling emptiness around Raijin began to fade. The chamber of the Temple of

Reflection reappeared, and Raijin found himself standing once more before the ornate mirror, his reflection staring back at him.

But the reflection was different now. It was no longer the image of a god weighed down by fear and doubt. It was the image of a god who had faced his inner demons and emerged stronger on the other side. Raijin's eyes were filled with a new sense of clarity and resolve, and his heart was lighter, free from the burdens that had held him back.

The spirits of the temple appeared around Raijin, their forms shimmering with a soft, ethereal light. They regarded him with expressions of approval and respect, their eyes filled with the wisdom of ages.

"You have passed the trial of the mind, Raijin," one of the spirits said, its voice filled with warmth. "You have faced your fears and doubts, and you have overcome them. You have gained a deeper understanding of yourself, and with that understanding comes great power. The power to shape your own destiny, to control your own fate."

Raijin nodded, feeling a deep sense of gratitude for the wisdom he had gained. "Thank you," he said, his voice filled with sincerity. "The trial was difficult, but it was necessary. I have learned much about myself, and I am stronger for it."

The spirits smiled, their forms beginning to fade into the light. "The journey is not over yet, Raijin," another spirit said. "But the wisdom you have gained here will guide you in the trials to come. Remember the lessons you have learned, and you will find the strength to overcome any challenge."

With that, the spirits disappeared, leaving Raijin alone in the chamber. The mirror before him had returned to its normal state, its surface smooth and reflective, but the power it held was still present, a reminder of the trial Raijin had just undergone.

Raijin took a deep breath, feeling a renewed sense of purpose and determination. The trial of the mind had been a difficult one, but it had given him the clarity and resolve he needed to continue his journey. He had faced his fears and insecurities, and he had emerged stronger on the other side.

As Raijin left the Temple of Reflection and stepped back into the cool, damp air of the forest, he knew that the battles ahead would still be challenging. The darkness had not yet been fully vanquished, and there were still many trials to come. But with the wisdom he had gained from the trial of the mind, Raijin felt ready to face whatever challenges lay ahead.

The world was still in need of protection, and Raijin was determined to fulfill his duty as the Thunder God. He would continue to fight for the balance of the world, for the protection of those he cared about, and for the future of all living beings.

And with that determination in his heart, Raijin set out on the next chapter of his journey, ready to face the challenges that awaited him, knowing that the power of the mind and the strength of self-awareness would guide him to victory.

—-

Chapter 12: The Return of the Forgotten Gods

A New Dawn of Unease

The sun rose over the lands Raijin, the Thunder God, had sworn to protect. The sky was clear, the world below quiet after the battles that had shaken it to its core. Yet, as Raijin stood on the balcony of his temple, looking out over the horizon, he felt an unease that he could not shake. This unease had been growing since his return from the trial of the mind, where he had faced his deepest fears and insecurities. Though he had emerged stronger, there was a new shadow on the horizon, one that did not come from the darkness he had been battling for so long.

It was an ancient shadow, one born from the deep recesses of time, from the memories of a world that had long since passed into history. Raijin could feel it in the air, a presence that was both familiar and alien, a force that resonated with the old magic that had once ruled the earth. It was a power that had been dormant for eons, forgotten by the world, but it was stirring now, awakening from its slumber.

Raijin knew that something was coming—something old, something powerful. But he did not know what it was or why it had chosen this moment to reemerge. The world had changed since the days of the old gods, and Raijin was now one of the most powerful deities, a protector of the balance between the forces of nature. Yet, the old gods had their own legacies, their own histories that had been lost to time, and Raijin could not ignore the feeling that these forgotten gods were returning, seeking to reclaim what they believed was theirs.

As the sun rose higher in the sky, casting its golden light over the land, Raijin turned away from the horizon and descended into his temple. He knew that he would need to prepare for whatever was coming, and that meant seeking out the ancient wisdom that had been passed down through the ages, the stories of the gods who had come before him, and the lessons of their rise and fall.

The Gathering of the Forgotten

Raijin's journey to uncover the truth began with a visit to the oldest library in the world, a vast repository of knowledge hidden deep within the mountains. The library was a place of great power and mystery, guarded by spirits of wisdom who had protected its secrets for millennia. The walls of the library were lined with ancient scrolls and tomes, each one containing the history of the world, the stories of the gods, and the lessons of the past.

As Raijin entered the library, he was greeted by the spirit of the head librarian, an ancient being of light and knowledge who had served the library since the dawn of time. The spirit's form was ethereal, its body shimmering with a soft, golden light, and its eyes were filled with the wisdom of countless ages.

"Raijin, Thunder God," the spirit said, its voice soft and melodic. "What brings you to the library of the ancients? What knowledge do you seek?"

Raijin bowed respectfully before the spirit, his heart heavy with the weight of the questions that had been plaguing him. "I seek the stories of the forgotten gods," he said, his voice filled with determination. "There is a shadow on the horizon, a presence that I cannot ignore. I believe the old gods are returning, and I must understand their history, their rise and fall, so that I may be prepared for what is to come."

The spirit nodded, its expression thoughtful. "The forgotten gods," it murmured, as if recalling a distant memory. "They were once powerful, revered by mortals and feared by their enemies. But time is a relentless force, Raijin. The world changes, and even the greatest of gods can be forgotten, their power diminished, their names lost to history."

The spirit gestured for Raijin to follow, leading him deeper into the library, where the oldest and most fragile scrolls were kept. "The stories of the forgotten gods are here," the spirit said, stopping before a large, ornate chest made of ancient wood and bound with iron. "These scrolls contain the history of their rise to power, their reigns, and their eventual fall. But be warned, Raijin—these stories are not just tales of glory and triumph. They are also cautionary tales, reminders of the transient nature of power and the importance of humility."

With a reverent hand, the spirit opened the chest, revealing the scrolls within. Each scroll was carefully preserved, the parchment yellowed with age but still legible. The spirit selected one of the scrolls and handed it to Raijin.

"This is the story of Koga, the Storm King," the spirit said. "He was once a god of great power, much like yourself, Raijin. But his pride and ambition led to his downfall. He sought to dominate the skies, to control the storms for his own purposes. But in the end, his arrogance led to his destruction, and he was forgotten by the world he sought to rule."

Raijin took the scroll and unrolled it, his eyes scanning the ancient text. The story of Koga was one of pride and ambition, of a god who had once been revered for his control over the elements but who had allowed his desire for power to consume him. Koga had believed that his strength was absolute, that he was invincible. But he had underestimated the forces of nature, and in his hubris, he had unleashed a storm so powerful that it had destroyed him and everything he had built.

As Raijin read the story, he felt a deep sense of foreboding. The parallels between Koga's story and his own were striking. Like Koga, Raijin was a god of the storm, wielding immense power over the elements. But unlike Koga, Raijin had always sought to use his power for the greater good, to protect the balance of nature rather than to dominate it. Yet, the story of Koga served as a reminder that even the most well-intentioned gods could fall victim to their own pride and ambition.

The spirit watched Raijin closely as he read, its eyes filled with a mixture of sadness and understanding. "Koga's story is but one of many," the spirit said. "There are others—gods who once ruled the earth, the sea, the sky, and even the underworld. They were all powerful in their time, but time has a way of humbling even the greatest of beings. Their names may have been forgotten, but their lessons remain."

Raijin nodded, his mind racing with the implications of what he had learned. "Thank you for this knowledge," he said, his voice filled with gratitude. "I will take these lessons to heart as I prepare for the challenges ahead."

The spirit smiled, its form beginning to fade as it returned to its duties within the library. "Remember, Raijin," the spirit said as it disappeared. "Power is fleeting, but wisdom endures. The forgotten gods may seek to reclaim their former glory, but it is the wisdom of the ages that will guide you in the trials to come."

With the scroll of Koga still in his hand, Raijin left the library, his heart heavy with the knowledge he had gained. The return of the forgotten gods was no longer just a possibility—it was an inevitability. And Raijin knew that he would need to confront them, not just with strength, but with the wisdom he had gained from their stories.

The Arrival of the Forgotten

The first sign of the forgotten gods' return came in the form of a storm—an unnatural, powerful tempest that swept across the land, darkening the skies and lashing the earth with torrential rain and violent winds. The storm was unlike any Raijin had ever encountered, its power raw and untamed, as if it were driven by a force beyond nature itself.

Raijin stood on the cliffs overlooking the sea, his eyes narrowed against the wind as he watched the storm approach. He could feel the presence of something ancient within the storm, a force that resonated with the old magic that had once ruled the earth. The storm was not a natural occurrence—it was a herald, a sign that the forgotten gods were awakening, returning to the world to reclaim what they believed was theirs.

As the storm drew closer, Raijin could see figures emerging from the clouds—shadows that took on the shapes of beings long since lost to history. These were the forgotten gods, the deities who had once ruled the earth but had been cast into obscurity by the passage of time. They were ancient, their forms twisted and gnarled by the centuries of slumber, but their power was still immense, their presence a testament to the forces that had shaped the world in ages past.

The leader of these forgotten gods was a figure that Raijin recognized from the scroll he had read in the library. It was Koga, the Storm King, the god who had once ruled the skies with an iron fist but had been destroyed by his own ambition. But Koga was not alone—he was accompanied by other gods, each one representing a different aspect of nature, each one seeking to reclaim their former glory.

There was Nami, the Sea Queen, a goddess who had once ruled the oceans with her powerful tides and currents. She had been worshiped by sailors and fishermen, revered for her ability to bring both bounty and destruction to the seas. But her power had waned over the centuries, and she had been forgotten, her name lost to the waves.

There was Hono, the Fire Lord, a god who had once commanded the flames that burned across the earth. He had been a force of both creation and destruction, his power feared and respected by all who lived in his domain. But like the others, his influence had faded with time, and he had been reduced to a mere shadow of his former self.

And there was Kage, the Shadow Weaver, a god who had once ruled the night, his power drawn from the darkness that enveloped the world. He had been a master of illusions and deceit, a god who thrived in the shadows, but his power had diminished as the world turned away from the old ways, and he had been forgotten.

These gods, once mighty and revered, had been reduced to obscurity by the passage of time. But they had not forgotten their former glory, and now they had returned, seeking to reclaim their place in the world, to challenge Raijin's reign as the protector of the balance.

As the forgotten gods approached, the storm intensified, the winds howling like the cries of a thousand lost souls. Raijin stood his ground, his heart filled with a mixture of dread and determination. He knew that this confrontation was inevitable, that the forgotten gods would not rest until they had tested his strength and resolve.

But Raijin also knew that this was not just a battle of power—it was a battle of legacy, of pride, and of the passage of time. The forgotten gods were relics of an age that had passed, beings who had once ruled the world but had been cast aside by the relentless march of history. Their return was not just a challenge to Raijin's power, but a reminder of the transient nature of all things, of the inevitability of change and the importance of humility.

As the forgotten gods descended upon him, Raijin called upon the power of the storm, his hammer crackling with lightning as he prepared to face them. The winds whipped around him, the sky darkening as the storm reached its peak, and Raijin knew that this would be a battle unlike any he had fought before.

The Clash of the Old and New

The first to strike was Koga, the Storm King. With a roar that echoed across the heavens, he summoned a bolt of lightning that split the sky, aiming it directly at

Raijin. The force of the lightning was immense, a display of power that would have shattered a lesser god. But Raijin was the Thunder God, the master of the storm, and he met Koga's attack head-on, his hammer absorbing the lightning and redirecting it back into the sky.

Koga snarled in frustration, his eyes blazing with anger. "You dare to challenge me, Raijin?" he bellowed, his voice filled with the fury of the storm. "I was the Storm King long before you were even born! The skies belong to me!"

Raijin met Koga's gaze with calm determination. "The skies belong to no one, Koga," he replied, his voice steady. "They are a part of the natural order, a force that must be respected and protected. You sought to control the storm for your own purposes, and that was your downfall. I will not make the same mistake."

Koga roared in anger, summoning another bolt of lightning, but this time Raijin was ready. With a swift motion, he brought his hammer down, unleashing a shockwave that dispersed the lightning and sent Koga reeling. The Storm King staggered back, his form flickering as the storm around him began to wane.

But Koga was not the only threat. Nami, the Sea Queen, stepped forward, her eyes glowing with the power of the ocean. With a wave of her hand, she summoned a massive tidal wave, sending it crashing toward Raijin with the force of a thousand storms.

Raijin braced himself, calling upon the winds to counter the wave. The air around him swirled with power as he directed the winds to push against the tidal wave, slowing its advance and eventually dispersing it into a spray of mist. Nami hissed in frustration, her form flickering like the waves on a stormy sea.

"You cannot stand against the power of the ocean, Raijin," Nami said, her voice cold and commanding. "The sea is eternal, its tides relentless. You are but a momentary ripple in its vast expanse."

Raijin shook his head, his eyes filled with resolve. "The sea is indeed powerful, Nami," he said. "But it is also a part of the natural order, a force that must be balanced with the others. You sought to dominate the seas, to bend them to your will, and that was your downfall. I will not make the same mistake."

Nami snarled, her form shimmering as she summoned another wave, but Raijin was ready. With a swift motion, he directed the winds to disperse the wave, sending it crashing harmlessly into the cliffs below. The Sea Queen staggered back, her power waning as the storm around her began to subside.

Next came Hono, the Fire Lord. With a roar of fury, he summoned a torrent of flames, sending them sweeping toward Raijin with the force of a volcanic eruption. The flames roared and crackled, the heat intense enough to scorch the earth and turn the air to ash.

But Raijin was undeterred. With a swift motion, he called upon the rain, summoning a deluge that extinguished the flames and sent steam billowing into the sky. The Fire Lord snarled in frustration, his eyes blazing with anger as his flames were doused by Raijin's power.

"You cannot extinguish the fire, Raijin," Hono bellowed, his voice filled with the fury of a thousand infernos. "The flames are eternal, their heat unquenchable. You are but a fleeting breeze in the face of their power."

Raijin met Hono's gaze with calm determination. "Fire is indeed powerful, Hono," he said. "But it is also a part of the natural order, a force that must be balanced with the others. You sought to control the flames, to use them for your own gain, and that was your downfall. I will not make the same mistake."

Hono roared in anger, summoning another torrent of flames, but Raijin was ready. With a swift motion, he called upon the rain once more, extinguishing the flames and sending the Fire Lord staggering back, his power waning as the storm around him began to fade.

Finally, there was Kage, the Shadow Weaver. With a sinister smile, Kage stepped forward, his form shifting and changing as he summoned the darkness to envelop Raijin. The shadows twisted and writhed, forming illusions that played on Raijin's deepest fears and insecurities, seeking to break his resolve.

But Raijin had faced the trial of the mind, had confronted his own fears and insecurities, and he was not so easily swayed. With a determined expression, he called upon the lightning, summoning a flash of light that cut through the shadows and dispelled the illusions. Kage snarled in frustration, his form flickering as the shadows around him began to retreat.

"You cannot banish the shadows, Raijin," Kage hissed, his voice filled with malice. "The darkness is eternal, its embrace inescapable. You are but a flicker of light in the face of its power."

Raijin met Kage's gaze with calm determination. "The darkness is indeed powerful, Kage," he said. "But it is also a part of the natural order, a force that must be balanced with the others. You sought to use the shadows to deceive and control, and that was your downfall. I will not make the same mistake."

Kage snarled in anger, summoning the shadows once more, but Raijin was ready. With a swift motion, he called upon the lightning, cutting through the darkness and sending Kage staggering back, his power waning as the storm around him began to dissipate.

The Wisdom of the Ages

As the forgotten gods staggered back, their power waning, Raijin stood tall, his hammer crackling with lightning as he prepared to deliver the final blow. But before he could strike, a voice echoed through the storm—a voice filled with the wisdom of the ages, a voice that resonated with the very essence of the natural order.

"Stop, Raijin," the voice said, its tone calm and commanding. "The forgotten gods are not your enemies. They are relics of an age that has passed, beings who once ruled the world but have been cast aside by the relentless march of time. Their return is not a challenge to your power, but a reminder of the transient nature of all things, of the inevitability of change and the importance of humility."

Raijin paused, lowering his hammer as he listened to the voice. The storm around him began to calm, the winds dying down and the clouds dispersing as the voice continued.

"Power is fleeting, Raijin," the voice said. "But wisdom endures. The forgotten gods may have sought to reclaim their former glory, but their time has passed. They have been humbled by the passage of time, their pride and ambition tempered by the lessons they have learned. Now, they seek not to challenge you, but to share their wisdom, to guide you in the trials to come."

Raijin looked at the forgotten gods, their forms flickering and fading as the storm dissipated. He could see the truth in the voice's words—the forgotten gods were not his enemies, but beings who had been humbled by the passage of time, who had learned the hard lessons of pride and ambition, and who now sought to share that wisdom with him.

With a deep breath, Raijin stepped forward, his expression calm and respectful. "I understand," he said, his voice filled with sincerity. "The power

I wield is not mine to control, but a part of the natural order that must be respected and protected. I will not make the mistakes of the past. I will use my power with humility, guided by the wisdom of those who came before me."

The forgotten gods nodded, their expressions filled with approval and respect. "You have learned the lessons we sought to teach, Raijin," Koga said, his voice filled with the weight of ages. "The power you wield is immense, but it is not eternal. It is a gift, a responsibility that must be handled with care. Remember this as you continue your journey."

Nami stepped forward, her eyes filled with the calm of the ocean. "The sea is eternal, but its tides are ever-changing," she said. "Remember that power, like the tides, is transient. It comes and goes, but wisdom endures. Use that wisdom to guide your actions, and you will maintain the balance of the world."

Hono nodded, his expression filled with the warmth of a dying ember. "The flames of power burn bright, but they can also consume," he said. "Remember that fire is a force of both creation and destruction. Use it wisely, and you will protect those you care about."

Kage stepped forward, his form shimmering with the shadows. "The darkness is not your enemy, Raijin," he said. "It is a part of the natural order, a force that must be balanced with the light. Remember that even in the darkest of times, there is always a glimmer of hope. Use that hope to guide your actions, and you will overcome any challenge."

With these words, the forgotten gods began to fade, their forms dissolving into the wind as the storm dissipated. Raijin watched them go, his heart filled with a deep sense of gratitude and respect. The return of the forgotten gods had been a test, not just of his strength, but of his wisdom, his humility, and his understanding of the transient nature of power.

As the storm cleared and the sun broke through the clouds, Raijin stood on the cliffs, looking out over the calm sea. The world was at peace, if only for a moment, and Raijin knew that he had learned a valuable lesson. Power was fleeting, but wisdom endured. The forgotten gods had shared their stories, their lessons, and their wisdom, and Raijin would carry that wisdom with him as he continued his journey.

The battles ahead would still be difficult, but with the lessons of the forgotten gods guiding him, Raijin knew that he would face them with humility, respect, and the understanding that true power came not from domination, but from balance and harmony.

And so, with the sun shining on the horizon, Raijin set out on the next chapter of his journey, ready to face the challenges that awaited him, knowing that the wisdom of the ages would guide him to victory.

Chapter 13: The Final Prophecy

Whispers of Fate

The battles had been many, the trials numerous, but Raijin, the Thunder God, had emerged victorious each time, his resolve unbroken and his power unchallenged. Yet, with every victory, he felt the weight of his responsibility grow heavier, as if the very forces of the universe were aligning for something greater, something inevitable. The world had been spared from darkness, the forgotten gods had imparted their wisdom, and yet there was an unease in the air, a sense that something final was looming on the horizon.

It began with a dream—a dream unlike any Raijin had ever experienced. In the dream, he stood on a desolate mountaintop, the sky above him swirling with dark clouds, the wind howling in his ears. The world was silent, save for the whispers that seemed to come from all directions, voices speaking in a language he could not understand. But one word was clear, repeated over and over again, echoing in his mind like a thunderclap: "Prophecy."

Raijin awoke with a start, his heart pounding in his chest, his mind filled with the lingering echoes of the dream. The word "prophecy" rang in his ears, a portent of something significant, something unavoidable. He knew that this was not just a dream, but a message—a call to action that he could not ignore. The time had come to seek out the truth, to uncover the final prophecy that would reveal his fate.

But Raijin also knew that the path to such knowledge was fraught with danger. Prophecies were powerful things, capable of shaping destinies and altering the course of history. To uncover a prophecy was to shoulder a burden of immense weight, a burden that could not be easily cast aside. Yet, Raijin was no stranger to burdens; he had carried the weight of the world on his shoulders for as long as he could remember. He would not shy away from this task, no matter the cost.

With determination in his heart, Raijin set out to find the oracle, the ancient being who was said to hold the secrets of time and fate, the one who could reveal the final prophecy that had been hidden from him until now.

The Journey to the Oracle

The oracle lived in a place beyond the reach of mortals, a place where time flowed differently, where the past, present, and future converged into one. It was a realm of shadows and echoes, a place that existed on the fringes of reality, known only to those who sought the deepest truths.

Raijin's journey to this realm took him through the heart of a vast desert, a barren wasteland where the sun beat down mercilessly and the sands seemed to stretch on forever. The air was thick with heat, and the ground beneath his feet was cracked and dry, a testament to the harshness of the environment. Yet, Raijin pressed on, his eyes fixed on the distant horizon, where he knew the entrance to the oracle's realm lay hidden.

As he journeyed deeper into the desert, the landscape began to change. The sky darkened, the sun fading behind a veil of clouds, and the air grew cooler, the heat of the desert giving way to a chill that seeped into his bones. The ground beneath his feet became softer, the sand shifting and swirling as if moved by an unseen force.

Finally, after what felt like days of travel, Raijin arrived at the entrance to the oracle's realm—a massive stone archway, carved from ancient rock and covered in symbols that pulsed with a faint, otherworldly light. The archway stood at the edge of a vast chasm, its depths shrouded in darkness, and beyond it lay the realm of the oracle, a place where time and space had no meaning.

Raijin stood before the archway, his heart heavy with the knowledge of what lay ahead. The oracle was a being of immense power, a creature who had existed since the dawn of time, and who had witnessed the rise and fall of countless gods and civilizations. To enter her realm was to step outside the boundaries of reality, to confront the truths that lay hidden in the fabric of the universe.

With a deep breath, Raijin stepped through the archway, feeling a strange sensation wash over him as he crossed the threshold. The air around him seemed to shimmer and warp, and for a moment, he felt as if he were floating, suspended in a void where time stood still. But then, the sensation passed, and he found himself standing on solid ground once more.

The realm of the oracle was a place of shadows and light, a vast, open space where the sky was filled with swirling clouds of mist and the ground was covered in a soft, glowing moss. The air was cool and still, and the only sound was the faint whisper of the wind as it moved through the mist. In the distance, Raijin could see a towering structure—a temple of ancient design, its walls covered in symbols and runes that glowed with a soft, ethereal light.

Raijin knew that this was the temple of the oracle, the place where the final prophecy would be revealed. With steady steps, he made his way toward the temple, his heart pounding with anticipation and a sense of foreboding. He knew that whatever awaited him inside would change the course of his destiny forever.

The Oracle's Revelation

The interior of the temple was vast and echoing, the walls lined with ancient tapestries and carvings that depicted scenes from the history of the world—battles between gods and monsters, the rise and fall of civilizations, and the cycles of life and death that governed all things. The air was thick with the scent of incense, and the light that filtered through the mist gave the space an otherworldly glow.

At the center of the temple stood a large, circular pool of water, its surface as smooth as glass, reflecting the light from the runes that adorned the walls. And at the edge of the pool stood the oracle—a figure draped in robes of deep blue, her face hidden beneath a hood that cast her features in shadow. Despite the obscurity of her appearance, Raijin could feel the immense power that radiated from her, a force that seemed to transcend time and space.

The oracle did not speak as Raijin approached, but he could feel her gaze upon him, her eyes piercing through the darkness of her hood. She raised a hand, gesturing for him to stand before the pool, and as he did so, the water began to ripple, the surface distorting as if moved by an unseen hand.

For a moment, there was silence, and then the oracle spoke, her voice soft but resonant, echoing through the temple like the tolling of a distant bell.

"Raijin, Thunder God," she said, her tone filled with a weight that made Raijin's heart ache. "You have come seeking the final prophecy, the truth that has been hidden from you until now. But know this—prophecies are not simple things. They are threads in the tapestry of time, woven into the fabric of the universe, and they carry with them the burden of knowledge, a burden that cannot be easily cast aside."

Raijin nodded, his eyes fixed on the rippling surface of the pool. "I understand, oracle," he said, his voice steady despite the uncertainty that gnawed at him. "But I must know. I must understand what the future holds, what my fate will be."

The oracle was silent for a moment, as if considering his words. Then she raised her hand once more, and the water in the pool began to glow, the light growing brighter until it filled the entire chamber. The ripples on the surface smoothed out, and the water became a perfect mirror, reflecting not just Raijin's image, but something more—something deeper.

As Raijin gazed into the pool, the reflection began to change. Images appeared in the water—scenes from his past, moments of triumph and despair, battles fought and victories won. He saw the faces of those he had loved and lost, the enemies he had defeated, the allies he had stood beside. But then the images shifted, and he saw something else—something he had not seen before.

He saw himself standing on the same desolate mountaintop from his dream, the sky above him filled with dark clouds, the wind howling in his ears. But this time, the scene was different. There was no whispering, no voices calling out to him. Instead, there was a presence—a figure standing before him, shrouded in shadow, its features obscured by the swirling mist.

The figure spoke, its voice a deep, resonant echo that seemed to come from the very earth itself. "Raijin," it said, its tone filled with a gravity that made Raijin's heart pound in his chest. "Your fate is sealed. The final battle is approaching, and you will face a choice—a choice that will determine the fate of the world. Will you accept your destiny, or will you forge your own path?"

The image in the pool shifted again, and Raijin saw himself standing at a crossroads—a literal fork in the road, with two paths stretching out before him. One path was straight and narrow, leading to a distant light that shone like a beacon in the darkness. The other path was winding and treacherous, filled with shadows and thorns, its destination obscured by the mist.

Raijin felt a chill run down his spine as he realized what the image represented. The straight path was the path of destiny, the path that had been laid out for him since the beginning of time. It was a path of certainty, of fulfillment, but also of finality. The winding path, on the other hand, was the path of choice, a path fraught with uncertainty and danger, but also with the possibility of forging his own fate.

The image in the pool faded, and the water returned to its smooth, reflective state. Raijin looked up at the oracle, his heart heavy with the weight of what he had seen.

"This is the final prophecy," the oracle said, her voice soft but filled with the weight of ages. "Your fate has been foretold, Raijin. The final battle will come, and you will face a choice—a choice between accepting your destiny and forging your own path. But know this—no matter which path you choose, the burden of knowledge will remain with you. The future is not set in stone, but it is shaped by the choices you make."

Raijin nodded, his mind racing with the implications of the prophecy. "What will happen if I choose to accept my destiny?" he asked, his voice filled with uncertainty.

The oracle was silent for a moment, as if considering his question. "If you choose to accept your destiny," she said finally, "you will fulfill the role that has been laid out for you since the beginning of time. You will face the final battle, and you will emerge victorious, but at a great cost. The world will be saved, but you will not. Your time will come to an end, and you will pass into the annals of history, remembered as a hero, but lost to the world."

Raijin felt a pang of sorrow at the oracle's words, but he knew that this was a possibility he had always known, deep down. "And if I choose to forge my own path?" he asked, his voice barely above a whisper.

The oracle's gaze was steady, her voice filled with both hope and caution. "If you choose to forge your own path," she said, "you will defy the prophecy, but the future will become uncertain. The final battle will still come, but its outcome will be unknown. You may succeed, or you may fail, but the burden of that choice will be yours alone to bear. The path will be difficult, fraught with danger, but it will be yours to walk."

Raijin was silent for a long moment, his mind reeling with the weight of the decision before him. The prophecy had revealed his fate, but it had also given him a choice—a choice between accepting the path that had been laid out for him and forging his own destiny. Both paths carried their own risks, their own burdens, and Raijin knew that whatever choice he made, it would shape the future of the world.

Finally, Raijin looked up at the oracle, his expression calm and resolute. "Thank you for revealing the prophecy to me," he said, his voice steady despite the turmoil within him. "I will take this knowledge to heart as I prepare for the final battle."

The oracle nodded, her form beginning to fade as the light in the temple dimmed. "Remember, Raijin," she said as she disappeared into the mist. "The future is not set in stone. It is shaped by the choices you make. Choose wisely, and you will find the strength to face whatever comes."

With those final words, the oracle was gone, and Raijin was left alone in the temple, the weight of the prophecy heavy on his shoulders.

The Burden of Knowledge

As Raijin left the temple and made his way back through the desert, his mind was filled with the images he had seen in the oracle's pool. The final prophecy had revealed his fate, but it had also given him a choice—a choice that would determine the course of the final battle and the future of the world.

The burden of this knowledge weighed heavily on Raijin's heart. He had always known that his journey would lead to a final confrontation, but the revelation that he would have to choose between accepting his destiny and forging his own path was a burden he had not anticipated. Both paths carried immense risks, and Raijin knew that whichever choice he made, it would have far-reaching consequences.

As he walked through the desert, the sun setting on the horizon, Raijin reflected on the lessons he had learned throughout his journey. He had faced countless challenges, battled powerful enemies, and gained the wisdom of the ages. But now, as he approached the final chapter of his story, he realized that the greatest challenge he would face was not one of strength or power, but of choice.

The thought of accepting his destiny and fulfilling the prophecy was both comforting and terrifying. It offered a sense of certainty, a path that had been laid out for him since the beginning of time. But it also meant sacrificing everything—his life, his future, his very existence. The world would be saved, but Raijin would be lost, a hero remembered in the annals of history, but gone from the world he had fought so hard to protect.

On the other hand, the thought of forging his own path was both exhilarating and daunting. It offered the possibility of defying fate, of shaping his own destiny, but it also meant stepping into the unknown, facing the final battle without the assurance of victory. The path would be difficult, filled with uncertainty and danger, and the burden of that choice would be his alone to bear.

As the sun dipped below the horizon, casting the desert in a deep, orange glow, Raijin knew that he would need to make his decision soon. The final battle was approaching, and the choice he made would determine the fate of the world. But he also knew that he could not rush this decision. He would need to reflect, to weigh the risks and rewards of each path, and to choose with both his heart and his mind.

The desert stretched out before him, a vast, empty expanse that seemed to mirror the uncertainty of the path he faced. But Raijin was not afraid. He had faced the trials of the gods, the darkness of the underworld, and the shadows of his own mind. He had emerged stronger each time, and he would do so again.

With the burden of knowledge heavy on his shoulders, Raijin continued his journey, knowing that the final prophecy had given him a choice—a choice that would define not just his fate, but the fate of the world. And whatever choice he made, he would face it with the strength, wisdom, and resolve that had carried him this far.

The Wisdom of the Ancients

As Raijin journeyed back to his temple, he found himself reflecting on the wisdom of the ancients, the lessons he had learned from the gods who had come before him. The forgotten gods had shared their stories, their rise and fall, and the transient nature of power. The oracle had revealed the final prophecy, the choice between accepting destiny and forging one's own path.

These lessons had shaped Raijin's journey, guiding him through the trials and tribulations he had faced. But now, as he prepared for the final battle, he knew that he would need to draw upon that wisdom more than ever. The choice before him was not just a matter of fate, but of understanding the nature of time, the cycles of life and death, and the balance between accepting what is and striving for what could be.

The ancients had understood the importance of this balance, the need to respect the natural order while also recognizing the power of choice. They had known that the future was not set in stone, but was shaped by the actions and decisions of those who walked the path of life. Raijin had seen this truth in the stories of the forgotten gods, in the teachings of the oracle, and in his own journey.

As he neared his temple, Raijin felt a sense of clarity begin to form in his mind. The final prophecy had revealed his fate, but it had also given him the power to choose, to shape his own destiny. The choice before him was not just a matter of accepting fate or defying it, but of understanding the nature of time and the role he played in the grand tapestry of the universe.

Raijin knew that he could not shy away from this choice, that he would need to face it with both humility and resolve. The final battle was coming, and the choice he made would determine not just his own fate, but the fate of the world. But he also knew that he was not alone—he carried with him the wisdom of the ancients, the lessons of the gods who had come before him, and the strength of his own convictions.

With the final prophecy weighing on his mind, Raijin entered his temple, the familiar surroundings giving him a sense of comfort and peace. He knew that the time to make his choice was drawing near, but he also knew that he was ready. The journey had been long and difficult, but it had prepared him for this moment, for the final chapter of his story.

And whatever choice he made, Raijin knew that he would face it with the courage, wisdom, and strength that had defined his journey from the very beginning.

Chapter 14: The Battle for the Heavens

The Calm Before the Storm

The final prophecy had revealed itself to Raijin, the Thunder God, and with it came the knowledge that the ultimate battle was inevitable. The heavens themselves seemed to hold their breath as the forces of light and darkness gathered their strength, preparing for the final confrontation that would determine the fate of the celestial order. Raijin knew that this battle would be the culmination of everything he had faced and learned throughout his journey—every victory, every loss, every lesson would be put to the test in this epic struggle.

In the days leading up to the battle, the world was eerily quiet. The storms that had once raged across the skies were now still, the winds calm and the clouds motionless. It was as if nature itself was waiting, anticipating the clash that was to come. Raijin spent these days in deep reflection, preparing himself not just physically, but mentally and spiritually for what lay ahead.

The final battle would not be fought on earth, but in the heavens—a realm where the laws of the physical world did not apply, where the forces of light and darkness clashed in a never-ending struggle for dominance. It was a realm that existed beyond time and space, a place where the very fabric of reality was woven from the energy of the universe itself.

Raijin knew that he would not face this battle alone. The allies he had gained throughout his journey—the mythical beasts, the spirits of nature, the forgotten gods—had all pledged their support, and they would stand beside him in this final confrontation. But Raijin also knew that this battle would test him in ways he had never been tested before. It would push him to the limits of his power, his courage, and his resolve. And in the end, it would be his choices, his sacrifices, and his willingness to stand up for what was right that would determine the outcome.

The morning of the battle dawned with a blood-red sky, the sun barely visible through the thick clouds that had gathered on the horizon. Raijin stood at the edge of the celestial plain, his hammer in hand, his eyes fixed on the distant horizon where the forces of darkness were beginning to gather. The air was thick with tension, the silence almost deafening as the two sides prepared to clash.

Raijin took a deep breath, feeling the familiar surge of energy as the power of the storm flowed through him. He knew that this would be the battle to end all battles—the struggle between good and evil, light and darkness, order and chaos. And he knew that whatever the outcome, the world would never be the same again.

The Gathering of Forces

As the forces of light and darkness gathered on the celestial plain, Raijin could feel the tension in the air, the anticipation of the coming conflict. On one side stood the forces of light—celestial beings of immense power, their forms glowing with a brilliant light that seemed to banish the shadows around them. These were the guardians of the heavens, the protectors of the celestial order, and they had been called forth to defend the realm against the encroaching darkness.

At the head of these forces stood Raijin, his hammer crackling with lightning, his eyes filled with determination. Beside him stood his allies—the mighty griffins, the fierce dragons, the majestic phoenixes, and the other mythical beasts who had pledged their support. The forgotten gods were there as well, their forms shimmering with ancient power, their eyes filled with the wisdom of ages. They had all come to stand with Raijin, to fight for the preservation of the celestial order.

On the other side of the plain, the forces of darkness were gathering—an army of shadowy beings, their forms twisted and grotesque, their eyes glowing with a malevolent light. These were the forces that sought to overthrow the celestial order, to bring chaos and destruction to the heavens. They were led by a dark entity, a being of immense power and malice, who had been waiting for this moment for eons.

This entity was known as the Shadow Lord, a god of darkness who had once ruled the heavens before being cast down by the forces of light. He had been biding his time, gathering his strength, and now he had returned to reclaim what he believed was rightfully his. His form was shrouded in darkness, his eyes burning with a fierce, unholy light. He was the embodiment of chaos, the antithesis of everything Raijin stood for.

As the two armies faced each other across the plain, the air was thick with tension, the silence almost unbearable. The forces of light stood tall and resolute, their eyes fixed on the enemy before them, while the forces of darkness writhed and twisted, eager for the battle to begin.

Raijin knew that this battle would not be like any other he had fought. The stakes were higher, the enemy more powerful, and the outcome more uncertain. But he also knew that he had no choice but to fight. The heavens were at stake, and the celestial order hung in the balance. He could not allow the forces of darkness to prevail.

With a deep breath, Raijin stepped forward, raising his hammer high above his head. The air crackled with energy as the power of the storm surged through him, and the sky above rumbled with the sound of distant thunder.

"For the heavens!" Raijin cried, his voice echoing across the plain. "For the celestial order! For the light!"

With a roar, the forces of light surged forward, their weapons gleaming in the dim light as they charged toward the enemy. The forces of darkness responded in kind, their twisted forms surging forward with a cacophony of hisses and snarls.

And so, the battle for the heavens began.

The Clash of Light and Darkness

The clash between the forces of light and darkness was nothing short of cataclysmic. The sky above was torn asunder as lightning flashed and thunder roared, the ground shaking with the force of the conflict. Celestial beings and dark creatures collided with a fury that shook the very foundations of the heavens, their weapons clashing with a sound that echoed across the celestial plain.

Raijin led the charge, his hammer crackling with lightning as he struck down one dark creature after another. His movements were swift and precise, each strike of his hammer sending shockwaves of energy through the air. He fought with a determination born of necessity, knowing that the fate of the heavens rested on the outcome of this battle.

Beside him, the griffins soared through the air, their sharp talons tearing through the ranks of the enemy. The dragons unleashed torrents of fire, their flames consuming the dark creatures in a blaze of light. The phoenixes dove from the sky, their radiant feathers glowing with a brilliant light that seared the shadows from the battlefield.

The forces of light fought with everything they had, their resolve unbreakable as they clashed with the forces of darkness. But the enemy was relentless, their numbers seemingly endless as they pressed forward, their twisted forms writhing and twisting in the dim light. The Shadow Lord himself was a force to be reckoned with, his power unmatched as he cut a swath through the ranks of the celestial beings, his dark energy corrupting everything it touched.

Raijin knew that he would need to confront the Shadow Lord directly if there was to be any hope of victory. The battle was fierce, and despite the strength of his allies, the forces of darkness were gaining ground. The Shadow Lord was the source of their power, and as long as he remained, the darkness would continue to spread.

With a surge of determination, Raijin pushed through the ranks of the enemy, his hammer blazing with lightning as he made his way toward the Shadow Lord. The dark entity stood at the center of the battlefield, his form towering over the chaos, his eyes burning with a malevolent light.

"Shadow Lord!" Raijin shouted, his voice cutting through the din of battle. "Face me!"

The Shadow Lord turned, his eyes narrowing as he focused on Raijin. A low, sinister laugh echoed from within the darkness that shrouded him, and he stepped forward, his form shifting and writhing as he moved.

"Raijin," the Shadow Lord said, his voice a deep, resonant echo that seemed to reverberate through the very air. "So, you have finally come to face your fate. You are a fool to challenge me. The heavens will fall, and there is nothing you can do to stop it."

Raijin met the Shadow Lord's gaze with unwavering determination. "I will not allow you to destroy the heavens," he said, his voice filled with resolve. "I will fight with everything I have to protect the celestial order. You may be powerful, but you are not invincible."

The Shadow Lord's laugh was cold and mocking. "You are but a child playing at being a god, Raijin," he sneered. "You do not understand the true power of the darkness. It is eternal, unyielding, and it will consume everything in its path. You cannot hope to defeat me."

Raijin tightened his grip on his hammer, his eyes blazing with determination. "I do not need to defeat you alone," he said. "I have the strength of my allies, the wisdom of the ancients, and the power of the storm. Together, we will stand against the darkness, and we will prevail."

With those words, Raijin charged forward, his hammer raised high as he unleashed a bolt of lightning that struck the Shadow Lord with the force of a thousand storms. The air crackled with energy as the two beings clashed, their powers colliding in a blinding flash of light.

The battle between Raijin and the Shadow Lord was nothing short of titanic. The sky above roared with the sound of thunder as lightning flashed and fire rained down from the heavens. The ground shook with the force of their blows, each strike sending shockwaves of energy through the air.

Raijin fought with everything he had, his movements swift and precise as he struck at the Shadow Lord with all the power of the storm. But the Shadow Lord was relentless, his dark energy corrupting everything it touched, his power seemingly endless as he pressed the attack.

For a moment, it seemed as though the Shadow Lord might overpower Raijin, his dark energy overwhelming the Thunder God's defenses. But Raijin refused to give in. He drew upon the strength of his allies, the wisdom of the ancients, and the power of the storm, and with a mighty roar, he unleashed a surge of energy that sent the Shadow Lord reeling.

The forces of light rallied around Raijin, their spirits lifted by his determination and strength. The griffins, dragons, and phoenixes fought with renewed vigor, their attacks coordinated and precise as they pushed the forces of darkness back. The forgotten gods lent their power to the battle, their ancient wisdom guiding the forces of light as they pressed the attack.

But the Shadow Lord was not defeated yet. With a roar of fury, he unleashed a wave of dark energy that swept across the battlefield, knocking Raijin and his allies back. The darkness spread like a poison, corrupting the very air and ground, and for a moment, it seemed as though all was lost.

But Raijin refused to give in. He knew that this was the final battle, the ultimate test of everything he had learned throughout his journey. He could not afford to falter now, not when the fate of the heavens hung in the balance.

With a surge of determination, Raijin stood tall, his hammer blazing with lightning as he called upon the power of the storm. The sky above responded to his call, the clouds churning and swirling as a massive bolt of lightning arced down from the heavens, striking the ground with a deafening roar.

The lightning struck the Shadow Lord, the force of the impact sending him reeling. The dark energy that had spread across the battlefield began to dissipate, the shadows retreating as the light of the storm banished them from the heavens.

Raijin pressed the attack, his hammer blazing with energy as he struck at the Shadow Lord with all the power he could muster. The forces of light rallied around him, their attacks coordinated and precise as they pushed the forces of darkness back.

The Shadow Lord let out a roar of fury, his form flickering and fading as the light of the storm overwhelmed him. The forces of darkness began to retreat, their twisted forms crumbling to dust as the light of the storm banished them from the battlefield.

And then, with a final, blinding flash of light, the Shadow Lord was gone. The darkness that had once threatened to consume the heavens was banished, the celestial order restored.

The Cost of Victory

The battle was won, but the cost had been great. The celestial plain was scarred and battered, the ground littered with the remains of the fallen. The forces of light stood victorious, but their numbers had been greatly diminished, their spirits weary from the struggle.

Raijin stood at the center of the battlefield, his hammer resting at his side, his eyes filled with a mixture of relief and sorrow. The battle had tested him in ways he had never imagined, pushing him to the limits of his power, his courage, and his resolve. But in the end, he had emerged victorious, the celestial order preserved, the heavens saved from destruction.

But the victory had come at a cost. Many of his allies had fallen in the battle, their forms lying still and lifeless on the ground. The griffins, the dragons, the phoenixes, and the forgotten gods—all had fought with everything they had, but not all had survived the struggle.

Raijin felt a deep sense of sorrow as he looked upon the fallen. They had given their lives to protect the heavens, to stand against the darkness, and their sacrifice would not be forgotten. But the weight of that sacrifice weighed heavily on his heart, a reminder of the cost of the battle, the price of victory.

As Raijin stood in the midst of the battlefield, the sky above began to clear, the clouds parting to reveal the light of the sun shining down upon the heavens. The light was warm and comforting, a reminder that the darkness had been banished, that the celestial order had been preserved.

But Raijin knew that the battle was not truly over. The final prophecy had revealed that he would face a choice—a choice between accepting his destiny and forging his own path. The battle had been won, but the choice still lay before him, and the burden of that choice weighed heavily on his shoulders.

As the sun continued to rise, casting its light across the celestial plain, Raijin knew that he would need to make his decision soon. The fate of the heavens, the future of the celestial order, rested on the choice he would make. But he also knew that whatever choice he made, he would carry with him the lessons he had learned throughout his journey—the importance of courage, sacrifice, and standing up for what was right.

With the weight of the battle still heavy on his heart, Raijin turned and began to walk toward the edge of the battlefield. The forces of light followed him, their spirits lifted by the victory they had won, but also tempered by the losses they had suffered.

And as they walked, Raijin knew that the final chapter of his story was yet to be written. The battle for the heavens had been won, but the journey was not yet over. The choice still lay before him, and the future was uncertain.

But whatever the future held, Raijin knew that he would face it with the strength, courage, and resolve that had carried him through the battle for the heavens. The lessons of the ancients, the wisdom of the forgotten gods, and the power of the storm would guide him as he made his choice, as he forged his own path, as he shaped the future of the heavens.

And with that knowledge, Raijin stepped into the light of the rising sun, ready to face whatever challenges lay ahead.

—-

Chapter 15: The Thunder God's Legacy

A Moment of Reflection

The battle for the heavens was over, the forces of darkness vanquished, and the celestial order preserved. The sun shone brightly over the realm of the gods, its warm light a symbol of the peace that had been hard-won. Raijin, the Thunder God, stood on the highest peak of the celestial mountains, looking out over the vast expanse of the heavens. The winds were gentle, carrying with them the scent of the sea and the song of distant birds. The world was at peace, but within Raijin, there was a storm of emotions.

The battle had taken a toll, not just on the heavens, but on Raijin himself. He had seen allies fall, had felt the weight of every decision, and now, in the aftermath, he was left to grapple with the legacy he would leave behind. The final prophecy had offered him a choice—a choice that would determine not only his own fate but the fate of the world he had fought so hard to protect. Now, standing on this peak, with the world spread out before him, Raijin knew that it was time to make that choice.

But first, he needed to reflect. He needed to understand the full weight of his journey, the lessons he had learned, and the legacy he would leave behind. The world had changed since the beginning of his journey, and so had he. The young god who had set out to prove his worth had become a leader, a protector, a hero. But with that transformation came the realization that every action, every choice, had consequences—consequences that would echo through the ages.

As Raijin stood on the peak, he felt the presence of the spirits of past heroes—the warriors, gods, and legends who had come before him, who had shaped the world with their actions, and whose stories had been passed down through the generations. These spirits were his predecessors, the ones who had faced their own trials, their own battles, and who had left their own legacies. They were here now, in this moment, to guide him, to offer their wisdom as he made the final choice that would define his legacy.

The Spirits of the Past

The first spirit to appear was that of Koga, the Storm King. His form was tall and imposing, his eyes filled with the same fierce determination that had defined him in life. But there was also a softness to his gaze, a sense of understanding and acceptance that had come with the passage of time.

"Raijin," Koga said, his voice like the rumble of distant thunder. "You have done well. You have faced challenges that would have broken even the strongest of us, and you have emerged victorious. But now, the time has come to decide what kind of legacy you will leave behind."

Raijin nodded, his eyes meeting Koga's. "I have fought many battles, Koga," he said, his voice filled with a mix of weariness and resolve. "I have protected the world, preserved the celestial order, but I cannot help but wonder what it was all for. What will remain after I am gone?"

Koga smiled, a deep, knowing smile. "Legacy, Raijin, is not about the battles we win or the power we wield. It is about the impact we have on those who come after us. It is about the stories that are told, the lessons that are learned, the memories that are kept alive. Your legacy will not be defined by your victories, but by the way you have inspired others, by the way you have shaped the world with your actions."

As Koga's spirit faded, another spirit appeared—a woman with flowing hair the color of the ocean, her eyes a deep, calm blue. It was Nami, the Sea Queen, who had ruled the oceans with both benevolence and power.

"Raijin," Nami said, her voice like the gentle lapping of waves against the shore. "You have stood at the crossroads of fate and made difficult choices. But remember, a true legacy is one that endures, that flows like the currents of the sea, touching everything it encounters. Your actions have ripples, and those ripples will be felt for generations to come."

Raijin nodded, absorbing her words. "But how can I be sure that the choices I make now will lead to a lasting legacy?" he asked.

"You cannot," Nami replied softly. "No one can. The future is ever-changing, like the tides. But if your actions come from a place of love, of wisdom, of a desire to protect and nurture, then your legacy will endure. It will be passed down, like a story told by the fire, a tale that grows and evolves but never truly fades."

With that, Nami's spirit faded, and another figure took her place—a figure shrouded in shadows, his form shifting and flickering like the night itself. It was Kage, the Shadow Weaver, the god who had once ruled the darkness but had learned the importance of balance.

"Raijin," Kage said, his voice a whisper that seemed to come from all directions at once. "You have walked the line between light and darkness, and you have done so with great care. But the legacy you leave behind is not just in the light; it is in the shadows, in the places where others fear to tread. Your actions have shown that even in the darkest of times, there is always a glimmer of hope. That is your legacy—the light in the darkness."

Raijin looked at Kage, his mind filled with the weight of the choices he had made. "But what if the darkness returns? What if my legacy is not enough to keep it at bay?"

"The darkness will always be there," Kage replied, his form flickering like a dying flame. "But it is the light you leave behind that will guide others through it. Your legacy is not just about what you have done, but about what you have inspired others to do. It is about the strength you have given them, the courage to face the darkness and find their own way through it."

Kage's spirit faded, and Raijin was left alone once more, the words of the spirits echoing in his mind. Each had offered their wisdom, their perspective on what it meant to leave a lasting legacy. And as Raijin stood there, the sun rising higher in the sky, he began to understand that his legacy was not something he could control or dictate. It was something that would grow and evolve on its own, shaped by the stories that were told, the memories that were kept alive, and the actions of those who came after him.

The Final Choice

With the wisdom of the spirits guiding him, Raijin knew that the time had come to make his final choice—the choice that had been revealed to him in the final prophecy. The heavens were at peace, but the question of his own fate remained. Would he accept the path that had been laid out for him, fulfilling his destiny and passing into the annals of history as a hero remembered for his deeds? Or would he forge his own path, defying the prophecy and embracing the uncertainty of the future?

Raijin knew that this was not just a choice about his own fate—it was a choice about the kind of legacy he wanted to leave behind. The prophecy had shown him that by accepting his destiny, he would save the world but at the cost of his own life. He would be remembered as a hero, but he would no longer be there to guide and protect the world he had fought so hard to preserve.

But by forging his own path, he would be taking a risk—a risk that the world might fall into chaos without the certainty of the prophecy. Yet, it would also allow him to continue to shape the future, to guide the next generation, and to ensure that his legacy was one of ongoing growth and change.

Raijin stood at the peak of the celestial mountains, the wind whispering in his ears, the sun casting long shadows across the land. He knew that whatever choice he made, it would have far-reaching consequences. But he also knew that he could not make this decision out of fear or doubt. He had to make it from a place of wisdom, of understanding, of love.

He closed his eyes, letting the memories of his journey wash over him—the battles he had fought, the allies he had made, the lessons he had learned. He thought of the spirits of the past, of the wisdom they had imparted, and of the future that lay before him, a future that was still unwritten.

When he opened his eyes, Raijin knew what he had to do.

Forging a New Path

Raijin raised his hammer, the symbol of his power, and called upon the storm one last time. The sky above responded, the clouds churning and swirling as lightning flashed and thunder rumbled. But this time, the storm was not a force of destruction—it was a force of renewal, of change.

With a single, decisive motion, Raijin brought his hammer down, striking the peak of the mountain with a thunderous crash. The impact sent a shockwave through the heavens, a pulse of energy that resonated through the very fabric of reality. The storm above roared in response, the winds howling, the lightning flashing in brilliant arcs across the sky.

But as the storm reached its peak, something remarkable happened. The clouds began to part, the lightning fading into a soft, gentle glow. The winds calmed, the thunder quieted, and the sky above cleared, revealing a brilliant, star-filled expanse.

Raijin lowered his hammer, a sense of calm settling over him. The storm was over, and with it, the final prophecy had been fulfilled—not by following the path laid out for him, but by forging his own. He had chosen not to accept the finality of destiny, but to embrace the uncertainty of the future, to continue to shape the world in ways that were still to be discovered.

The legacy he would leave behind would not be one of a hero who had saved the world and then disappeared into legend. It would be the legacy of a god who had chosen to remain, to continue to guide and protect, to pass down his wisdom to the next generation. It would be a legacy that lived on, not just in the stories that were told, but in the actions of those who followed in his footsteps.

Raijin knew that this path would not be easy. The future was uncertain, and there would be challenges, dangers, and sacrifices yet to come. But he also knew that he was not alone. The spirits of the past, the allies he had made, the wisdom he had gained—all of these would be with him as he continued his journey.

As the first rays of the morning sun broke over the horizon, Raijin looked out over the heavens, a sense of peace and resolve filling his heart. He had made his choice, and with it, he had shaped his own destiny. The future was unwritten, but it was filled with possibility, with hope, with the promise of new beginnings.

The Eternal Story

As the years passed, the story of Raijin, the Thunder God, became a legend—a tale told by the fire, passed down from generation to generation. It was a story of courage, of sacrifice, of the battle between light and darkness, and of the choices that defined a hero's legacy.

But it was also a story of hope, of the enduring power of legacy, and of the impact that one's actions can have on the world. The tale of Raijin was not just a story of a god who had fought great battles, but of a god who had chosen to remain, to guide, to protect, and to inspire.

The heavens changed over time, as all things do. New gods rose, new challenges emerged, and new stories were written. But the legacy of Raijin endured, a constant presence in the hearts and minds of those who came after him. His story was not one of finality, but of continuity, of a legacy that lived on through the actions of those who had been inspired by his example.

And so, the story of Raijin was passed down, from parent to child, from teacher to student, from one generation to the next. It became a part of the fabric of the world, a tale that was told not just as a history, but as a source of wisdom, of guidance, of inspiration.

The spirits of the past continued to watch over the world, their wisdom guiding those who sought it. And among them, Raijin stood, not as a distant legend, but as a living presence—a god who had chosen to remain, to continue to shape the world with his actions, to ensure that his legacy was one of enduring impact.

The story of Raijin, the Thunder God, was an eternal story—a story of courage, of sacrifice, of hope, and of the enduring power of legacy. And as long as there were those who remembered, who told the tale, who carried his wisdom in their hearts, Raijin's legacy would never fade.

The heavens would change, the world would evolve, but the legacy of the Thunder God would endure, an eternal presence in the story of the world.

And so, the story continues...

—-

Don't miss out!

Visit the website below and you can sign up to receive emails whenever Patrick William Lee publishes a new book. There's no charge and no obligation.

https://books2read.com/r/B-A-FLRYB-XXGTE

Did you love *The Legend of the Thunder God*? Then you should read *The Phoenix King*[1] by Patrick William Lee!

The Phoenix King: unfolds the epic journey of a mythical ruler born from the Sacred Flame, destined to balance life and death. As he navigates trials of fire and confronts ancient evils, the Phoenix King must harness the Eternal Flame's power to restore harmony to his kingdom. From battling gods to merging with a dark counterpart, his quest reveals profound truths about sacrifice and renewal. This compelling saga weaves a tale of legacy, resilience, and the eternal cycle, inspiring generations to embrace balance and the unending dance of creation and destruction.

---

1. https://books2read.com/u/bQXlaZ

2. https://books2read.com/u/bQXlaZ

About the Author

Patrick William Lee is a renowned author celebrated for his enchanting tales of magic and wonder. Specializing in the genres of fairy tales, folk tales, legends, and mythology, Patrick weaves stories that transport readers to fantastical realms where the impossible becomes reality. With a deep love for folklore and a talent for crafting timeless narratives, his books captivate the imaginations of readers young and old. When he's not writing, Patrick enjoys exploring ancient forests, studying mythical creatures, and sharing his passion for storytelling with audiences around the world. His works continue to inspire and delight, leaving a lasting impact on the world of literature.